THE GIRLS OF THE FRENCH QUARTER

Also by John Burton Thompson

Born to be Made
Hot Blood
Kiss or Kill
One More for the Road
Swamp Nymph

THE GIRLS OF THE FRENCH QUARTER

JOHN BURTON THOMPSON

CUTTING EDGE

ISBN-13: 978-1-952138-53-9

Published by
Cutting Edge Books
PO Box 8212
Calabasas, CA 91372
www.cuttingedgebooks.com

CHAPTER 1

FAVRA AND HER FRIENDS

"I SUPPOSE you could say the party was a success," murmured Aaron Festival as he watched the smoke curl from his cigarette.

Favra McMullin hesitated as she stroked a stiff brush through her tawny hair. "Yes … I suppose so. Why do I give them and why do people come?"

"You're bored and given to foolish thoughts. The thoughts give birth to foolish questions. I might ask one. What do you get out of parties?"

"I get a laugh once in awhile. I can watch the human animal at work after the fourth drink and I avoid being alone."

"Your laugh is brittle," he replied. "It lacks spontaneity. The human animals you gather here are so supersophisticated that it takes alcohol to wash away their veneer. Then, instead of being honest animals, they become human swine. As for being alone, you don't hate that. You could be married, you know, if you'd stop lying about your age."

She whirled around, a satiny leg skidding through the slit in the robe, shimmering like a shaft of the purest Elgin marble touched with pink tan. Casually she drew the silk over it and then frowned. "What makes you say that?"

"My dear, we all may be asses of various sorts but occasionally we display a little intelligence. Do you still insist that you are only twenty-two?"

"It's the truth. Naturally I insist."

He sighed. "Forgive me, but none of us believes it."

"I shall die of grief."

"Please do not be sarcastic."

"Please do not be a fool. Let's not quarrel. By the way, how is it that after everyone has gone home I find you in my bedroom watching me brush my hair?"

"I'm a friend of yours," he said easily, wetting his red lips. "I enjoy privileges not accorded the herd because you consider me harmless. And because I'm considered harmless, I have just seen what some dozen of your guests would give a handsome sum to see."

"What?"

"A leg. A leg of such appalling beauty that were I not an esthete, I should probably be drooling and pawing at you right at this moment, trying to achieve the goal toward which your two legs form twin highways of a material that surpasses description. A magic mixture of marble, ivory and gold."

She laughed and slid the leg out again for his inspection. "You will make a vain woman of me, Aaron."

"You were a vain woman some seconds after your father's genes shook hands with your mother's chromosomes or some such genetic chaff…the actual mechanics of it escapes me."

"Tell me, what happened to your genes and chromosomes?"

"Some say one thing and some say another. Some say I was traumatized at a tender age, but when I look at my somewhat effeminate figure, I wonder if they aren't, to use one of their favorite terms, guilty of over-simplification. Men like me, whose faces are beardless and whose voices are given to squeaking at inconvenient moments, are not supposed to care for women. Yet I find them to be the absolute epitome of beauty…the beautiful ones, that is. I can feast my eyes on them endlessly."

"Just your eyes?"

He shrugged. "If you are attempting to make me ashamed of myself, please do not waste your time. I am what I am and that is the end of it. I have made peace with the bad gods and I tilt on even terms with the good ones."

"Yet you have never touched me."

"That's because you're so young, though I do believe you are a liar to the extent of several years. I am not a prowler in the night bent on frightening children no matter how beautiful or desirable they are."

"But I just never have been able to feel that you are a man. You never frighten me, you never revolt me, even though people say odd things about you."

"I am an artist who creates images beyond human conception... in my own mind. I take you—the color, the life of you—and I paint you on my canvas. You have no conception of the beauty thus produced."

"How do I appear on your canvas?"

"Oddly enough you appear to be what you are. A surpassingly beautiful woman; passionate, but who has not yet tasted passion; moderately intelligent, but not enough to make her revolting."

She watched him closely, her eyes half closed. He was slightly built with blond curly hair, sensuous lips, and skin as fine as her own. She felt a ripple of excitement course through her. What sort of man was he? She could feel his eyes on her as they traveled from her bare leg up to where the neck of her robe dipped enticingly away from the full globes of her breasts. With an effort she threw off the feeling and drew the robe over her leg.

"And," he continued, "you have sudden surges of Victorian prudery."

She flushed. "What should I do, undress?"

"Naturally. You're not afraid of me and you give the impression of being a woman of the world. What would you have to lose?"

"Everything," she replied.

"On the contrary. I am not a stallion nor do I look upon you as a mare. Some day some man will, and you'll revel in it."

"I'm not a mare," she flared.

"Will you undress?"

"Is that what you stayed for?"

"Among other things. I shall count the night lost if you refuse."

Without thinking she stood suddenly, allowed the robe to slide from her shoulders. She was curved with such deft sculpture that his hissing inhalation could be heard across the room. If she expected a sudden backwash of modesty, she was disappointed. Pride in the glorious length of her body began to suffuse her. Pride in her long flawless legs, the proud uplift of her breasts and the narrow lines of her waist. Her breath came faster as she saw him rise and approach her slowly, eyes bright, lips parted. His fingers touched her shoulders and traveled lightly downward, while his head bent as though bowing to divinity; his purpose sent a hot charge of electricity rocketing through her. She was on the couch without knowing how she got there, conscious only of the magic joy of his lips as they wove about her a spell of utter delight. Her throat fluttered with small senseless cries and her hands clutched him spasmodically.

He sat up and took a deep breath, then closed his eyes tightly and relaxed against the back of the couch, allowing her gradually to return to normal.

"You see," he murmured, "you have nothing to fear from me, at least not to the point of losing *everything*."

"Aaron…"

"Yes?"

She sat up, her body crying out so loudly that she wondered if he could hear it. "Aaron, take me and crush me in your arms… please, Aaron…"

"I mentioned not long ago that you'd need a stallion. I'm not he…"

Her fingers clutched his blond hair, frenzied movement took possession of her. She was suddenly afire with such dizzying ecstasy that her mouth opened. His soft fragrant palm over her lovely lips prevented an outcry. She lay bonelessly on the couch, her arms and legs askew like those of a sleeping kitten, awkward and yet sublimely poetic because there can be no awkwardness in true beauty.

"Sleep well, my overwrought but so lovely little mare," he said softly. "Your stallion will appear by and by."

Her sleep that night started out heavy and dreamless but she woke, at four, chilled and stiff on the couch. Shivering, she went to her bath, and took a hot shower. Dawn found her still awake.

The sun was painting the drab roof of the St. Louis Cathedral a most unchurchly color when she finally arose and walked to the tall mirror where she considered herself gravely through smoky gray eyes. A magic mixture of marble, ivory and gold, he had said. A flush rose to her skin, painting it a delicate pink beneath its tan. She moistened her full, passionate lips and touched their corners with her fingertips, smoothing away imaginary wrinkles. She shook her head till her hair danced about the flawless perfection of her shoulders then resolutely turned away from her narcissistic study and dressed. Usually she ate a breakfast of café au lait and hot square doughnuts at the French Market two blocks from her apartment. Throwing a cape over her shoulders, she brushed her hair furiously till it glowed, a mass of tawny gold. She left the apartment and walked down the narrow, cobbled street with its ornate iron balconies, passed the Cabildo, the Cathedral, across Jackson Square to the French Market. She took a table under the awning. "Mornin', Miss Favra," said a bent little man with bright bird-like eyes and sharp features.

"Good morning, Jesse. How many doughnuts can I have this morning?"

He cocked his head. "Lemme see … Have a party last night?"

"Yes."

"Eat much supper?"

"Didn't eat any."

"Gee…that's bad, drinkin' on an empty stomach. I'll slip some extra cream in your coffee and bring you four doughnuts. But go easy on the sugar. Well, there's the Professor. It ain't many mornin's you beat him up."

The Professor was a small neat man dressed in black alpaca, his cuffs frayed but clean and starched, his tie merely a black string with the ends as even as if they had been measured.

"Ah…Good morning, Favra, my dear, and Jesse! A lovely morning, is it not?" He spoke with precision, stroking his neat white moustache.

"Mornin', Professor…the same?"

"The same." He took a seat at Favra's table. "And, of course, you are looking like an affront to all the world's ugliness as usual…" The Professor stopped suddenly and peered at her, his blue eyes alive and penetrating. "You are not merely beautiful this morning, you are positively lambent, if I may be bold and trite at the same time."

She flushed. "You see entirely too much, Professor. Thanks for the lift though. I can always depend on you to feed my ego."

"Desiccated applause from a dead branch. You've done better…recently…or I miss my guess."

Her flush heightened. "How long have we been eating breakfast together, Professor?"

"Eh…oh, about a year I'd say. Why?"

"In that time you've learned practically everything about me. I know absolutely nothing about you, except that you are a man of insight. I don't even know your name."

He smiled, showing dimmed but still attractive teeth. "Do not envy me my anonymity, my child. I have done a terrible thing to an honorable name, so in deference to the name, I prefer to be known as Professor…. Alice, come on and have breakfast with us."

Alice could have been seventy or a hundred and ten. Her black dress was clean and pressed but ragged and unattractive. She shuffled forward and took her seat carefully, trembling and holding onto her stick. She threw her cape back and let the sun shine on her snow-white locks. "We three," she said, her voice low and sweet, "seem to get together often. How is the lovely Favra this morning?"

"Fine, Alice. What'll you have for breakfast?"

"The same. I can remember when what I eat now wouldn't have amounted to hors d'oeuvre. Age dulls many of the senses."

"But not all," averred the Professor gallantly. "You are beautiful as usual, Alice."

"And you're the same liar as yesterday and the day before."

The old man laughed. "Favra has been needling me about my past."

"I told him he knew everything about me and that he has never even told me his name."

"Maybe it's best that way," murmured Alice. She caught Jesse's eye and nodded in answer to his raised eyebrow. Soon, smoking, hot rectangular doughnuts and huge mugs of coffee with boiled milk lay before them.

"I know her name," complained the Professor breathing on his coffee, "but little else that my wits didn't tell me."

"No one is making small of your wits," said Alice as she broke a doughnut.

"You can say that again," put in Favra. "I'll give you a thumbnail sketch though. I come from Texas. I love New Orleans because of its wickedness that amounts to almost a virtue, its smells, good food, easy good fellowship and live-and-let-live atmosphere. I'm twenty-two and my great uncle who died a number of years ago left me a whole battalion of oil wells. I have no people that I admire, so I bore good people, like you and Alice, for companionship."

"I was a great lady once myself," said Alice without rancor, pulling bits of doughnut from the larger piece. She had no teeth. "Now I totter up and down the Quarter and people feel sorry for me, give me money."

"I was a professor," said the little man shortly. "I dare say I still could be."

Favra laughed. "My story was longest, Alice's next and you, Professor, brushed us off, like a bellhop in a swank hotel."

"Leave the old fool to his hermitage," said Alice. "You look different this morning, Favra."

"Don't say that," darted the Professor. "It makes her blush."

Favra proved his assertion by flushing attractively. "Does either of you know why?"

Alice looked at the Professor who met her eyes. "You tell her," he said. "A woman knows how to put those things much better than a man."

She smiled. "It is obvious, dear. You didn't sleep alone last night."

Favra did not blush this time and the alarm that flared in the Professor's eyes prompted her to allay his fears. "I'm not offended, Professor. After all, this is the Quarter, you know. I'm single and fair game. I'll admit that something of an extraordinary nature happened to me but I'm not saying what."

"This ancient female," said the old man acidly, "is as blunt as the edge of a superannuated meat clever. I could have done a better job myself."

"A more devious job," Alice corrected, "one in which the same thing would be said in a full tide of euphemism. At my age that is unnecessary."

Favra laughed. "Here, I'll take the check this morning."

"Indeed not," said the Professor snatching it out of her hand. "You've bought breakfast for a week."

"But I'm able to buy it …"

"Oh, let the old fool pay for it," said Alice. "He also enjoys fourflushing on occasion."

"That is not so," the Professor replied with heat. "I dislike being a sponger."

"You can still afford your pride? I can't and it doesn't bother me in the least. Either of you may pay for my breakfast. Do you think it's an accident that I'm here at the same time every morning?"

The Professor took his turn at flushing. "I didn't mean to be offensive, Alice, I meant…"

"I know very well what you meant. What makes you think I took offense? The only thing that can touch me now is death. I avoid the subject with a great deal more fervor than the very young because it has meaning for me."

Favra became immediately interested. "What does death mean to you?"

The crone shrugged. "Very little, actually, except that it is the station where one gets off the train. I find a number of old people are like me. They regret what they missed and fret over it. The only things we regret are the temptations we successfully resisted."

"I did not think of you as a woman who read Oscar Wilde," said the Professor. "I must say that it lacks morality … the quotation, I mean."

Alice grinned broadly, exposing healthy red gums. "I'll Oscar you again. 'Morals are all right but they have such low entertainment value!'"

The Professor looked at her through narrowed eyes. "You say the most astounding things sometimes!"

Favra leaned forward. "What would you do if you were my age, with my money and your present wisdom?"

The old woman's eyes narrowed as she gave the girl a long scrutiny. "I'd have the city eating out of my hand, if I had a free one. Lacking that I'd make them eat out of the gutter. I'd collect

scalps like old lady Bosworth collects Eastern pottery. I'd worship at the shrine of love and I'd taste everything that promised
flavor. Having money, I could pick and choose, so I'd be hard
to please. I'd strive to miss nothing that was consistent with my
own conception of good taste and my health. I'd be a dog every
now and then, to make being human a contrast. I'd do everything at least once."

"You," accused the Professor, "could be burned at the stake
for what you advocate."

"She should be put on a white horse up in the square beside
General Jackson," put in Favra, her cheeks glowing.

Back at the apartment she found T'ling, her colored girl, hard
at work polishing the living room floor. T'ling claimed to be part
Chinese, a claim which her delicate face with its obviously ori-
ental cast supported. She was willowy, clean-limbed, figured like
a houri, possessed of a moral code that occasioned her little loss
of sleep. She had great brown eyes fringed with silky jet lashes.
She could easily have been the pet of a wealthy man rather than
a houseworker.

The thought struck Favra as she walked in and put her
purse on the blond wood coffee table. "T'ling, why do you work
for me?"

The answer was swift. "Because I like you. You're not getting
tired of me, are you?"

"Oh, for heaven's sake, no. ... I just wondered. You're too
good-looking to be doing housework."

T'ling smiled showing even white teeth. "So, you're wondering about that, too?"

"I certainly am. It seems to me that you could do better."

"I could but I wouldn't be as free as I am. I tried it once."

"You did? ... What happened?"

"He got drunk and tried to beat me and I popped a butcher
knife in his belly ..."

"But…"

"Yes'm. I could have taken care of the rough stuff all right, but he wanted me right there all the time. He came when he got good and ready but I had to be there all the time. I used to go crazy from nothin' to do."

"What happened when you knifed him?"

T'ling laughed, a silvery tinkle of a sound. "He was a prominent man and couldn't afford to have anything get out. He went to a hospital and stayed there till he got well. He received a lot of newspaper space because he said he'd been held up and fought the robber."

Favra gasped. "Not Jackson Darrow?"

T'ling lowered her head. "I didn't mean to give that away. I didn't know you'd been here that long."

"I haven't, but didn't you know that Mrs. Linda Deforest is his daughter?"

T'ling's hand went to her mouth. "Oh, Lord. The good-looking Mrs. Deforest that is always making eyes at men?"

"That's the one."

"Jesus, but it's a small world…I hope I've answered your question."

"I'll say you have and it was really none of my business. I think of you more as a friend than a servant, T'ling, and you may ask me any question you care to. If I don't want you to know I'll tell you so."

The girl looked at her steadily. "How come there never is but one pillow messed up on your bed?"

"Because I'm the only one who sleeps in the bed."

T'ling laughed softly. "I guess you told *me*."

"I didn't mean it that way…I guess…Oh, hell, I don't know. I couldn't truthfully answer. Maybe that's why I said it."

"Nothing has ever really touched you, I guess."

"Up till last night it hadn't…" Favra's hand went quickly to her mouth. She hadn't meant to talk about Aaron.

"I left Mr. Festival here," said T'ling slowly. "You don't want to get mixed up with a man like that."

"Why?"

"Because it ain't ... isn't natural." T'ling was very careful of her speech when she thought it necessary.

"Do you think there's any harm in Mr. Festival?"

"No'm, I didn't mean that. It's just sort of ... well, you *might* get to like it."

T'ling continued her waxing and Favra sank into deep thought. There had been something missing last night. She had wanted to be hurled about. She had wanted a hairy chest against her, the manly smell of a strong body, muscles that crushed. She snapped back to the present and sat up, beads of sweat on her upper lip. She went to the roof and, arranging her screens, stripped naked and allowed the hot sun to beat down on her skin. Twenty minutes later she anointed her body with a rich oil, enjoying the sensation of her hands moving over her slippery limbs.

As she came down the steps. T'ling looked at her.

"You could be arrested," she breathed. "I've never seen anything like you."

Favra stood on the bottom step and posed for a second.

"Miss Favra ... will you go with me?"

"Go with you ... where?"

"There's something you ought to see. I promise you'll be all right but it might shock you."

"Shock me! ... How absurd! ..." Favra's skin tingled at the thought. "I ... I mean I'd just watch ... wouldn't I?"

"Oh, yes'm. People go to these places ... some of them to ... well, learn things. It's owned by a woman ... and it's helped people, people that don't know anything."

"When will we go?"

"We can go tonight. You don't have to change any of your plans. You can leave right after it's over and it only takes an hour ... maybe a little more."

"Very well. I'll go." Suddenly Favra felt excited. Was it to be one of those "things" she had heard about? No, T'ling wouldn't take her to something horrible like that. Whatever it was it would be good.

That afternoon Favra was invited to a party at the studio of Ecco Tying, pronounced "Tyang," and the invitation was delivered in person by Linda Deforest who seemed to combine evening and afternoon drinking into one perpetual tipple.

"Darling," said the elegant Linda as she walked in with Aaron Festival, "I am simply a desert. Please have that little maid of yours whip up something tall and strong. Then I'll tell you something." She sank languidly into a chair. Aaron came over, took Favra's hand, examined it minutely, nodded and sat down. "Something blocked my reconstruction of the hand and it worried me. I was afraid it would turn out to be deformed."

Linda opened her eyes. "What are you doing now, sculpturing?"

"You wouldn't understand, my dove," said Aaron as he accepted a highball from T'ling. "Here is your transfusion. May there be many more."

"Hear, hear," she applauded as she took the slim aluminum tumbler from the tray and caressed its frosted sides with her fingers. She drank thirstily then lit a cigarette with her fingers. "Ecco insists that I bring you to his party tonight, Favra. In fact, he said if you didn't come he'd call it off. He even threatened to go to bed."

Aaron lit a thin cigarette. "Ecco's threats to go to bed become a bore at times."

"Go to bed? ... Maybe I'm behind the times but what about going to bed? A lot of people do."

"Ecco," he said with a wry smile, "has managed to get it aired about that he went to bed once in a fit of pique and remained there a year. There are cases of snide doubt that any such thing happened. But that's his story."

"You're mean," pouted Linda. "Ecco is an artist, very highly tuned, tense, and emotional."

"I've seen a five-dollar violin highly tuned," retorted Aaron blowing a smoke ring.

"You're just jealous because he's more eccentric than you are."

"My dear woman, since when did eccentricity become a virtue? Or an excuse for exhibitionism? Please, Linda, you drivel when you attempt to wax intellectual."

She pouted. "I guess you think *you're* an intellectual."

"I am what I am."

She shot him a malevolent glance. "You *do* have your uses."

"So do the meanest of us … including you. Just what they are in your case is yet to be discovered."

"Here … you two. Cut it out. So I take it that unless I go to the party, Ecco'll go to bed."

"So he says, darling. Please don't disappoint us."

"Favra just might have something to do … like polishing her shoes or taking a stroll in the park. If she does, she'd be well advised not to let this party interfere."

"I don't know what you have against him," flared Linda. "I have never seen *you* miss one of his parties."

"You've never seen me miss any party," he retorted.

"There is always liquor of sorts and occasionally a beautiful woman."

Linda turned to Favra. "May I tell him you'll be there, darling?"

"Tell him I'll come but I'll be late. I might not get there at all. It would be amusing to see if he'd really go to bed."

"But," protested Linda, "he couldn't write …"

"Small loss," murmured Aaron.

"Ecco is a successful novelist, my dear," Linda said nastily. "What is your success … to date?"

"It has been said that I'm surpassingly successful just being Aaron Festival. As for Ecco being a novelist ... I laugh, although I do not feel like laughing. He writes what he calls esoterica—nothing but filth. No reputable publisher will touch it. He gets it published by a vanity house and sells it under the table at fabulous prices. Successful, no doubt, but he is a swine and rarely bathes."

Linda bounced to her feet. "I'm leaving you here, Aaron. Don't you dare follow me."

"I wouldn't think of it," he said gently putting out his cigarette. "I followed you in because you got to the door first."

She left in a huff slamming the daffodil yellow door so hard the windows rattled.

"Why do you badger her?"

"She irritates me. In another ten years, after youth has gone, she will be a fishwife, shrieking and babbling, still trying to make men notice her."

"Aaron, did you ever ..." Favra stopped, her face stinging.

He raised a well-shaped eyebrow at her. "You needn't be shocked. I have. She has beautiful points but she doesn't know it. To be unaware of beauty of self is a worse crime than being unable to observe it in others. Awareness, my dear, is the only quality we possess over the animals, ministerial braying to the contrary notwithstanding."

Her skin irritated, pulses pounding and face hot with turgid blood, Favra stood up. Her voice was unnatural. "I'm going to bathe ... I'm going out early. I know you ... will excuse me."

He stood up with fluid grace. "I'll excuse you."

CHAPTER 2
HOUSES OF SOME REPUTE

THEY ARRIVED at the house that, due to shadows and lack of light, Favra could tell little about from the outside. Inside it was even darker but the carpet under her feet was rich and the chair soft. "I'll come back after I've seen someone," promised T'ling.

She sat back and tried to relax but she couldn't take her eyes from the fantastic shadows cast by a dim light somewhere outside the house, intruding misty arms through the windows. She drew her fingertips over the fine fabric with which the chair was upholstered realizing that it, too, was rich and expensive, wishing with all her might that T'ling wouldn't take long. There was utter silence in the big room nor did much street noise filter in, noise she would have welcomed to help dispel the feeling of complete aloneness. She wasn't a fearful person but she shared most of humanity's discomfort in the face of the unknown.

When a hand touched her shoulder she barely kept from screaming. "You can come now." Trembling she allowed herself to be led through dim carpeted corridors till at last they started down a flight of steps. Down, she thought; I was expecting up. Where can this be leading? She clutched T'ling's hand for comfort, reaping additional moral support from a strange red glow that seemed to come from some secret place, like a trickle of water, yet covering everything. The walls seemed red from its ruby glow and its effect on the colored girl's skin was beautiful in a savage way. They came to a room that was aflame with the red light, so much so that Favra could see a woman seated at a small table.

"Has T'ling told you what you will see?" asked the woman in measured accents.

"No. I think I have something of an idea." The woman was arresting to say the least, her jet black hair falling to her shoulders in deep soft waves, complementing her ivory skin, both being touched by the sullen red light in a way that made Favra's pulse beat faster.

"You will not see anything like this anywhere else but I warn you it will be a shock."

"I came prepared for a shock."

"That is good. If you have scruples we prefer that you leave, because twenty-five dollars is a stiff price to pay for being shocked."

"If I have scruples I can control them," said Favra handing her the money.

"Miss McMullin, what you are about to see is nothing more or less than nature at work. If it is beautiful, then it is because nature is beautiful. If it is ugly, nature can also be ugly. You may go in now. It is almost time."

Strangely moved, Favra followed T'ling through a door into a large room that was almost dark, being slightly illuminated by the same red emanation that she had noticed while coming through the corridors. Other people were there, grouped in a number of little stalls formed by hanging curtains of dark heavy velvet which afforded complete privacy except from the front. She and T'ling sat on some cushions.

In the center of the room she could barely discern a black circular hole in the ground and while she was still wondering what it was, a soft red glow rose slowly from it. Out crept a crimson finger of flame of such scarlet color as to remind her of a railroad signal torch. It rose higher till it flickered two feet from the ground and showed the faces of others across the room like pale blobs of butter. From a distance, or so it seemed, there came now the muted mutter of drums so soft that Favra felt the vibration in her breast before she could actually hear it. Gradually the vibrations increased till they made her throat tickle and her blood course faster. There was something about the sound of such undressed savagery that she could feel the tingle of gooseflesh down her spine. It seemed to soak into her body and infect every nerve and muscle, calling back through the dim ages since her last ancestor stamped about a red blaze in the depths of some primeval forest to the rhythm of skins stretched over hollow logs, beaten frenziedly with blunt sticks. Her breath came faster, her torso swaying to the heady beat that had now risen in volume till it seemed to mingle with the fierce glow of the fire, like smoke with steam, and to fill the room with its thundering cadences.

A lithe beautiful girl raced through the shadows in the background and stood before the fire her arms upraised and her back arched. She was of mixed blood, bronze-skinned, divinely formed, and nearly naked. About her waist was an ankle-length skirt of sorts made of shimmery white cord, not too closely arranged, so that her strong dancer's legs showed through. She began to shift from one foot to the other, her slim body undulating with serpentine rhythm to the beat of the drums. Favra strained her eyes trying to see where they were located but as before she could only see the dim faces of the other spectators glowing redly in the light of the flame. Another girl raced from the shadows and joined the first one, similarly dressed looking almost like a twin except that her skirt was made of glossy red material instead of white.

A third and fourth girl, whose costumes were green and yellow, joined the group and it surrounded the fire, bodies caught in the drum beat like sinuous puppets answering its every order. They backed away and executed several simple but savagely fundamental steps that all ended in a quick exaggerated glance toward one side of the room. She could feel T'ling grow tense beside her, the girl looking fixedly in the direction that the dancers threw their glances. Favra, so tense that her back and shoulders ached, found herself also watching the spot with bated breath but without knowing why or what she expected. She was soon to see. A veritable giant of a man stepped from the darkness followed by three more who, for size at least, were his counterparts. Their only clothing was a skin-tight breech cloth that corresponded in color to the cord skirts worn by the girls. They advanced on the girls, their skins oiled and glistening in the light of the red flame, muscles rolling and slipping beneath the bronze of their hides with such smooth coordination that Favra caught her breath sharply, tingling from scalp to toes from the weird performance, wondering how it would end.

The men were as accomplished at the dance as the women and together they began to move about in a routine that might have been new when man first descended from the trees and began to walk upright. Faster and faster the drumbeats rataplaned from their hidden recess, having been joined by several reed instruments that sounded to her like oboes with a certain Far Eastern flavor. The dancers began to sweat from the fury of their exertions and now she began to notice something new. The dancers seemed to have ceased proceeding from any plan. They would lock in an embrace, the girl straining herself to her partner with a fury that sent her diaphragm into spasmodic contraction, then the man would disengage himself and dance in a circle seemingly to tease the girl. It soon became evident that the girls at least had forgotten why they were in the dim circle. Their eyes glassy, their hair dripping sweat, their breath rasping hoarsely they were striving to gain surcease from the terrific emotion the dance had built up. They began hurling themselves at the men, their intentions all too evident, being thrown about like rag dolls but coming back, their throats now delivering querulous little utterances, animal-like, frenzied, and avid.

"What makes them like that?" she asked in a tense whisper.

T'ling, as taut as a bow string, bent toward her without taking her eyes from the rapidly moving figures. "I don't know what they're using…maybe nothing. Some of the girls don't need anything…the ones that come from Haiti and Jamaica, they say they don't although I always thought they took something. They've been educated to voodoo and they can get into a state like that without much trouble. I used to get a little drunk and once I took a drink of some stuff a girl told me about that tasted like tea that was too strong. I'll never do it again, though."

Favra sat back weakly. As she did, one bronze giant stooped suddenly and picking his girl up in his arms dashed away from the light. In less than a minute the room was empty of dancers, the drums faded away and Favra heard a smothered cry that came from a spectator, then several different outbursts of nervous sobbing from people who had not been able to endure the strain.

"Come on, Miss Favra. I'll take you where you can see."

She stumbled into darkness behind T'ling, feeling that there were others coming along but not being certain of it.

Ten minutes later she allowed herself to be led through the house to the street where she stood trembling and mopping her face.

"Now you see what I mean when I say Mr. Festival isn't any good for a woman like you."

Favra nodded silently as she climbed into her car. "I'll take you home."

"No, m'am…"

"What?"

"I don't want to go home. You can put me down another place if you want to."

She mentioned an address and Favra eyed her queerly. "That's one of the best apartment houses in New Orleans."

"Yes'm."

"How will you ... I mean, will they let you in?"

"With a maid's uniform on who'd stop me?"

"Yes, I suppose so." She heaved a big sigh and relaxed bone-lessly against the upholstery for a moment before starting her car. "By the way, T'ling ... thanks. I think the trip was well worth the effort. I can see where people might learn a lesson all right if they had a little sense to start with."

"Yes'm. Plenty of people go there to learn things. Some just go for fun of course, but Madam ... well, the lady you talked to is mighty choosy about who she lets in. There were more big shots there tonight than you ever saw in one place. Some of them stayed."

"You ... you mean the men, I suppose?"

"Yes'm ... the men and some women, too."

She caught her breath, "T'ling ... no!"

"Yes, ma'm. When I was there the Madam had men on call at all times. They're fine-looking men, well built, healthy, and best of all, they don't talk. One tried to blackmail a woman once and he disappeared. Nobody knows what became of him. That's the only trouble she ever had."

"So you worked there, too?"

"Yes'm. It wasn't regular work. Just for a few hours three times a week, but the pay was good ..." T'ling's lilting laugh tin-kled ... "and it was fun."

Favra drew in a deep breath, started her car and pulled away from the curb. Twenty minutes later she pulled up before an apartment house that sat back from the street in a grove of great live oaks, lights burning discreetly at the entrance.

"This is a side of your life that I didn't know about," she said as the girl got out of the car. T'Ling's smile was vixenish and dimply.

"Don't many people know about it ... just three ... you, me, and him."

"How often do you come here?"

"Whenever I feel like it."

"Oh … he doesn't call you or anything?"

"No, ma'm. I just come to see him whenever I want to."

"How do you know he's in?"

"He mostly is. He gets off from work at five and unless the Madam calls him he'll be home."

"You met him … there?"

"Yes, ma'm." T'ling dimpled again. "There was a storm one night and the show was called off. He was called in earlier but the lady couldn't make it …" T'ling dropped her eyes. "We had a lot of time to kill and …" Her voice trailed off. "He's wonderful."

Favra drove off with a feeling of unreality possessing her. Not one single thing that had happened since seven o'clock could be true and yet she had seen it with her own eyes. Her mind went back to the little booth, the tiny red lamp and the sounds that had come from the room. She recalled the etched details of the girl's muscles strutted in agonized ecstasy, the transcendent delirium in her great dark eyes. She went suddenly weak and parked the car on a dimly lighted street while she tried to recover. She rested her face in her hands for a while, then she started the car again, feeling a little stronger and in better control of her emotions. She drove to Ecco Tying's studio and parked out in front for ten minutes while she debated the advisability of going in. She did not care for Ecco who worked so hard at eccentricity that he was offensive and irritating. Moreover, as Aaron had said, he did not appear to bathe often. His hair was long and unkempt, his teeth mossy and green, and his breath foul. Still it was considered proper to attend parties when people invited you. She frowned and opened the door to her car.

"I waited," said Aaron as he walked up with his peculiar mincing stride, "half hoping that you'd stay away and then we'd see if the great man would take to his bed."

"That's the most ridiculous thing I ever heard of," she murmured idly, her mind not on Ecco at all.

Aaron examined her curiously. "You appear distraught on the one hand and preoccupied on the other. I might add that it usually takes a complexity of emotions to achieve such an oddly suited pair."

"Please, I don't feel quite up to your particular brand of humor right at the moment."

"I loathe myself. What shall I be, debonair, serious, foolish, intellectual…"

"You might try being masculine," she said cuttingly.

"Dear me. Were I the least bit sensitive about such things I might successfully accuse you of striking a low blow."

"I'm sorry," she said in a voice that did not sound at all sorrowful, "but you irritate me at times. I didn't mean to indulge in personalities."

"Don't give it a thought. I could creep away and die, you know… but I won't, just to spite you."

"Oh, let's go in and face Ecco. We will become conspicuous out here gabbing on the sidewalk."

He waved his hand airily. "Precede me. I'll come along and see what Ecco has to drink."

She took a few of the steps up toward Tying's studio, stopped and faced Aaron who was following. "Aaron, why is it you never walk with a woman? You always walk behind her."

He raised his eyebrows expressively. "Why, didn't you know? To watch the music of their figures, of course. Yours, I might add, is a veritable concerto."

"Oh…" she snorted with irritation, climbed the rest of the way and pushed the doorbell. A leering Filipino let her in and took her things. "Misser Ecco be very plezz, Miss Favra, that you come."

"Never mind the chatter, you foreign excrescence." Aaron's snarl was that of a rather young puppy, making the tiny man chuckle and leer even more.

"Oh, yezz…" Aaron walked on into the combination living, work, and general utility room where some dozen people sat and stood about in various stages of intoxication. Linda had cornered a young man who displayed a notable sprinkling of acne, a spread of teeth the size of rice grains, but shoulders of commendable breadth. He was shooting glances about, half in fright, looking for a means of escape. Aaron walked to a sideboard that did double duty as a bookcase proper and bar. He sampled the bourbon, found it drinkable, sauntered mincingly to a stool in the corner and sipped his drink, watching with bright, intent eyes the music of all female behinds that happened to be moving.

Ecco, though not a painter wore a white smock of questionable cleanliness and when he saw Favra he lunged across the room, the tails of the smock lending the impression that he was gliding. He held out his hands and caught hers, the look in her eyes aborting a privately avowed intention of embracing her.

"Ah, the fabulous Favra…and why are you late? I have been…"

"Inconsolable," she supplied, setting him back for a second because it was the very word he had intended using.

"You're prescient," he breathed, caressing her hands and sending a shiver of revulsion over her. "That was the very word I'd have used if you hadn't said it for me."

"What's all this business of your threatening to go to bed if I hadn't come?"

He held himself up heroically. "I would have done that very thing," he said. "I simply *had* to feast my eyes on you. Do you realize it has been a whole day since I saw you?"

"Oh, come," she said in disgust. "Don't you think you're overdoing it a bit? Why don't you try going on a hunger strike or something? Gandhi used to get action that way."

A wave of sorrow passed over his face. "You're making fun of me. I bleed internally."

"Cheers," murmured Aaron from his corner. "External bleeding is no end messy and unsanitary."

Ecco directed a vitriolic glance at him, but turned back to Favra, only to find that she was not there.

She approached Linda and the youngster who was beginning to show signs of wear.

"Ecco wants to see you."

The boy watched his attacker go with undisguised relief. "Thanks," he said huskily. "We were already at her apartment for a nightcap."

"She doesn't waste much time. I'm Favra McMullin."

"Richard Cartwright Sayler the Third."

"Gosh ... all of that?"

He grinned. "All of it. One and Two are still alive."

Aaron came up and touched her on the arm. "Shall I erect a drink for you?"

"Yes, do. Make it double, triple, quadruple, or something. Fix it so it'll walk over here alone."

"Gad, but I'd like to know where you went before you came here. It must have been something."

"Run along and erect the drink," she said lightly, noticing with a little too much clarity that Sayler had several leaking acne pustules and any number of them that were ready to burst. Her stomach reeled and she turned away. "I saved your life," she tossed back. "I'll leave it to you now."

She could feel his eyes in her back as she walked across to where Aaron was busily making a drink. She doubted that she had been wise to interfere and Linda bearing down on her with thunder in her eyes intensified the conviction.

"Worm," she said venomously to Aaron, "did you put Favra up to that fabrication just so I'd lose my man?"

He tilted an eyebrow at her. "We caught seven, how many did you catch?"

"What?"

He shrugged, "You should, I think, go soak your head. The few times I've seen you sober you were endurable, however, that state is so seldom achieved."

Linda turned her back on him. "Favra, I don't think you're one bit nice and Ecco is furious and sulking in his bedroom. You'll have to go entice him out."

"Has he taken to his bed?" he asked maliciously, handing Favra her drink.

She ignored him, gasping and putting a finger to her lips. "That utter little bitch has my man ... Favra, I could murder you."

"Bitch she may be," said Aaron brightly, "but little she is not. It does appear that she could wait till she got him home."

"Who is she?" asked Favra, hoping to turn the conversation into better channels.

"She," answered Aaron lighting one of his thin Russian cigarettes, "is a dauber of limp, uninspired oils. Her name, I believe, is Bella Manana."

"My God," breathed Favra. "Ecco Tying and Bella Manana. As you say she seems to be making hay where Linda couldn't even make an impression."

"I think both of you are horrible ... and mean ... and, and, and, ... I hate you." Linda dabbed at her eyes and hurled herself away from them to flop pettishly in the first available chair and sob into a tiny handkerchief.

"I repeat," mused Aaron, "you are certainly letting a lot of this go over your head tonight. I don't suppose there's any chance you'd tell me what you did before coming here."

"Not a chance, son. Bella Manana is certainly pouring it on."

He tapped a length of ash on the floor and nodded. "If you'll observe, her shape has been compressed somewhat about the midsection giving the distinct impression of a light bulb. That means a boned girdle. Snaps off handily, though, no doubt. For breasts she has two great blobs of protoplasm that might successfully suckle a litter of bull pups, say a dozen to each one. Her waist is probably the only beautiful part of her. It is slim and her belly does not pouch."

Favra was at first irritated, changed her mind and laughed. "You are the damnedest man I ever saw."

"Her legs," he continued, "are passable but the thighs are probably stuffed to the point of clotting…. dimpling… revolting."

"Have you…?" Her eyebrows lifted questioningly.

"My dear, you crush me. The woman is undoubtedly dirty. No one could possibly have any other reason for taking a bath in Chypre."

"I thought the place seemed overpowered with it. All on her?"

"But of course. She trails it like a ship trails smoke. Hadn't you better go and entice Ecco from his bed?"

"No, he might try to entice me into it."

"And you wouldn't like that?"

"Oh, stop it. To quote you, the man seldom bathes… I'm afraid."

"Now, there is something that catches my eye," exclaimed the other.

"She's awfully young. Who did she come with?"

"Pimple Face, I think. Observe! Her skin is tender and thin, almost immature, I'd say. Her legs would be downy and as smooth as yellow satin. Her breasts are of the demitasse variety with strawberry tips. They could be made as hard as cold butter. Her throat is rich cream where the sun has touched it …"

"What, no hot fudge?"

"Oh, yes… although her youth and coloring would indicate that it would probably be quite light …"

Favra burst into a peal of incredulous laughter. "I'll say this for you, you never could be a bore."

"That is probably the best compliment I've had in years."

"Who is the character with the off-balance hair-do and the pirate's earring?"

"Oh ... don't you know? He makes figurines. No one has ever quite decided what they represent. In some five thousand words of unintelligible jargon he can tell you, though. Trouble is, you're no better off from having been told. Name of Lofton Kramm."

"He's the aloof type, eh?"

"Not necessarily. Linda, after two more drinks will attach herself to him and they will hie off to her apartment for the last game of baccarrat. He has a notable capacity, however. No man who can put away as much whiskey as he is entirely without virtue."

"I think I'll go rout Ecco from his pout."

"Rout from pout. You'll be a member of the colony yet, my dear."

She made a face at him and walked through the milling people and into the little hallway that led to the bedroom. She opened the door, her nostrils wrinkling with distaste from the effluvia of humanity that assailed her. Ecco's bedroom was a shambles. The bed was what might have been Eastern except that it was manifestly a box spring with no legs upon which the top mattress rested. The coverlet was mauve silk and the pillow looked as though it might have been used as a foot wiper. The walls displayed several lovely watercolors and one atrocious lithograph of a naked woman. The master stood looking tragically out of the window into a courtyard where a couple unable or unwilling to seek further cover were having fun in plain view of all who might choose to look. Noticing this, Favra found his tragics less convincing. "I've come to invite you to the party," she said brightly. "That is, if you can tear yourself from the free show long enough."

He started. "I, er ... don't know what you mean. I was staring blindly through the window blackly contemplating what the future would bring were you not by my side."

"Only the future can supply that little bit of information but I promise that it will."

"Don't make any hasty resolutions, Favra. What have I done to deserve a locked mind?"

"Let me ask you something. Why this sudden decision that I am necessary to your future?"

"I have been cogitating upon the matter ever since I first met you. I reached my decision last evening. I have a confession to make. I crawled up the fire escape and watched you undress in your bath."

Strangely, she was neither offended nor shocked. She was concerned with what else he might have seen. "And how long did you remain in your loathsome position?"

He faced her and ran his fingers through his lank hair turning it into further disarray. "Please don't be angry. I simply had to know."

"Know what?"

"What you looked like without clothes. I have seen all now. I could accept blindness with equanimity."

"Oh, drop dead! You sound like some fatuous school boy. How long did you remain on my fire escape?"

"Only long enough to drink my fill of your unclothed divinity. Then I left and I have been one great furuncle of love ever since."

"You have a full store of nauseous analogies," she said crisply, relieved that he had not stayed longer and seen more.

"Tell me that my passion shall not go for naught, tell me, Favra, ere I perish."

"Holy cow," she ejaculated in amazement. "How sticky can this thing get?"

He caught her suddenly in his arms. "I've got to have you … you're driving me mad, I tell you. Please do not resist me …"

His hands began to wander freely. "Turn me loose, Ecco, right now. I don't want to slap you but I shall with all my strength in one moment … I said let me go."

Suddenly she felt her arms pinioned from behind. "Take her, Ecco," cried Linda. "I've got her arms."

She felt his hands rasping against her skin and for one split second she almost screamed. That they could handle her she did not for a moment doubt, but after that first impulse she closed her lips and fought grimly. It was Linda who screamed, however, and released her with such suddenness that she fell to the floor hard with Ecco on top of her, still clawing at her, his eyes bright with the madness of his desire. Then he too yelled and rolled off and sat cursing on the floor. Linda leaned against the wall and sobbed brokenly, Ecco swore and fingered his behind while Aaron beamed beatifically at an enormous hatpin he held in his hand. "Bella has such quaint bonnets," he said to no one in particular. "I found at least one excellent weapon in its attic."

Favra leaped to her feet almost beside herself with fury now that the danger was past. She launched a kick that caught Ecco flush in the gullet sending him over backward gurgling and gasping, then she turned, snatched Linda from her wailing wall and with a full-armed swing knocked her sprawling on the pseudo-Eastern bed.

"Bravo," applauded Aaron. "I've seen more professional swings but rarely one more destructive. Do you suppose the Ecco will become a mere echo? From here he appears to be somewhat at a loss for air."

Ecco was indeed at a loss for air. Her hard-driven foot had done something to his gullet. His breathing was now touch and go, and his face had turned a repellant shade of grape.

"I don't give a damn if he chokes," snarled Favra searching for some slight evidence of returning truculence in either of them.

"That is all very well," he observed calmly. "I, however, having no madness in my brain will have to prevent this from becoming murder." He lifted the French phone and dialed. "Will you dispatch an ambulance to fifty-five-o-six St. Louis, please ... Yes, a man is choking on a foot." He cradled the receiver just as the first knock sounded on the door. He grinned and threw it open. People crowded in, all asking questions, with Bella saying above the noise, "I told you I heard screams and you wouldn't believe me … I told you … I told you."

"I make bold to suggest," murmured Lofton Kramm, "that someone aid Mr. Tying with his respiration, else this might easily turn into something tragic."

No one, it appeared, cared enough about Mr. Tying's breathing to do any such thing so Lofton with a shrug of his big shoulders bent over and manipulated Ecco's crushed trachea until he began to breathe easier and a little of the cyanosis left his face. A few minutes later an ambulance crew came in and loaded him onto a stretcher.

"I'd suggest someone retain this position with a helping hand," said Lofton. "Unless you do he'll choke."

One of the men nodded, replaced Lofton's hand with his own and they wheeled the injured man from the room.

"Well, I wanter know what happened," brayed Bella looking from Linda to Favra to Aaron.

"Let her tell you," said Favra who was a little calmer now, and Linda, taking this as a sign that she could get up, clambered shakily from the bed.

Lofton took one look at her and burst into a bellow of laughter. "Katie, what a mouse … Jesus." A mouse it was that no one had noticed because of her position on the bed and the dimness of the lights. She burst into a torrent of tears and fled the room leaving Aaron and Favra to explain what the disturbance was about.

"Now you can tell us," gurgled Bella sending off a gentle spray of spittle in her eagerness.

"I'm afraid you'll be disappointed," snapped Favra. "If you've had enough, Aaron, I'll drop you by your house."

"And you'll no doubt go in and spend a while," said Bella maliciously, balked and irritated.

"And what do you mean by that?" Favra asked, whirling about.

"Oh, the usual. I don't think it intelligent of you to pretend that you don't know what he likes to do to beautiful women."

"That's what you think, is it?"

"Yes, it is and I don't thin ..." Whatever it was that Bella did not think remained a mystery because Favra swung an open hand to her face with such force that she reeled drunkenly and sat with a crash in a chair, her right hand raised with unconscious drama to protect her face. Aaron stepped forward, deposited the hatpin in the hand and stepped back. "I return the stiletto none the worse for wear. One and all, a very good night. You, Bella, had better watch your language. Our Favra is in a lethal mood."

The car slid to a stop before a small house that stood relatively by itself for the Quarter. Its front was obscured by two gigantic camphor trees and several banana bushes, each bearing a purple flower the size of a grapefruit. Aaron stepped from the car. "Come on in and have a couple of drinks of good liquor. It'll make you sleep better."

"And make Bella right?"

"My dear, Bella was already right. Pray do not pretend otherwise and skid my opinion of your intellect into the cellar."

She sighed and stepped from the car. "I guess you're right but I don't think you're good for me."

He led her up the walk, produced a key and opened the door. "I shall be glad to point out where you're wrong when I have served drinks."

His home was a never-never land. Warm pastels and robust solid colors seemed this once to have something in common. His furniture was of no particular period, but in no instance was there a clash. A fine antique *escritoire* occupied a short dimensioned wall. The walls were pale blue and the ceiling a rich creamy yellow. His couch was very expensive and comfortable, with pillows of bright silk and several silk covered ottomans.

The walls were interrupted by paintings, some modern and some old, but all of them held intrinsic beauty, riots of lilting color or, quiet peaceful things that neither offended the eye nor intruded on the more florid moods of the others.

"Somehow," she murmured, "this place doesn't seem to be you at all. It is beautiful and you love beauty more than anyone I know…still…" She gnawed her lower lip and surveyed the living room again. He approached, bearing highballs in deep emerald green glasses on a rich but severely plain silver tray.

"Before one could make such a remark without fear of contradiction one would have to know a great deal more about me than you do. I am not a human to you. I am, to be vulgar, a trumpet flower. You know little or nothing of what really makes up Aaron Festival, the man." He said the last two words with a touch of irony.

"Does anyone?"

"No. People know of me just what I choose to let them see. I am not as bad as you might think and probably not as good as I think I am."

"I do like you a great deal."

"Why? Because I came to your rescue with a hatpin?" He chuckled. "It was the only thing I could pick up at a moment's notice. I would not exchange fisticuffs with Ecco. I could not in the name of manhood strike Linda, but I understand pricking a woman with a pin is not unchivalrous."

"No, that's not the reason. You…Oh, I don't know. You don't seem to offend me. You're thoughtful and actually kind sometimes. You irritate me but that's because I feel like laughing and the conventional in me dictates that I shouldn't."

"I shouldn't think you'd have any trouble overcoming that," he remarked dryly. "After all, you've shattered tradition rather thoroughly."

"I know it and part of the irritation comes from that. It doesn't bother me in the least and it should."

"Why?"

She sighed. "I knew you'd ask that, and of course I can't answer it. I give up."

"I did not bring you here to heckle you," he said softly. "I like you, which is why I treat you like a lady. You are a lady and a very fine one. The fact that you refuse to allow convention to render you husk dry is in your favor, not against you."

"You said you'd tell me why you are good for me … or why you are not bad for me."

"Oh, yes." He took a long drink and put his glass down. "To begin with, my delicately contrived little mare, you are in as little danger of becoming perverted as I am in danger of developing normalcy. About the worst thing I could do to you is give you an appetite for things which your stallion, whoever he might turn out to be, might not appreciate."

"You have awakened me," she told him frankly. "What do I do now?"

"Search for the stallion, several of them preferably, so you can pick and choose."

"Do you think you could be a little less blunt?"

"Not to you, my pretty. I've found that you can take it and you're such a treasure that I wouldn't dare break out a euphemism for you. I refuse to indulge in obscenities but on the other hand I will not dress things up for you."

She sighed again. "Now from feeling that you were bad for me I have come to think you are good for me … this drink is powerful."

"No accident," he assured her. "You need relaxing."

"May I take off my shoes?"

"You may take off everything if you desire."

She sat very still, the skin of her legs prickling as she felt his eyes upon her. Slowly she stood up and with a few simple movements stood clothed only in a pair of tight briefs and bra.

Later she lay limp and exhausted, sobbing without reason, the leather of the divan sticking to her skin like an adhesive. Gradually she regained control of her emotions, feeling a rush of resentment against him smoking his cigarette, cool, detached, and perfectly at ease. Suddenly she reacted to a tremendous urge and told him where she had been earlier in the night, down to the last exciting detail. As she talked he grew interested and when she had finished he was leaning forward, his eyes bright and excited.

"Do you mean to tell me that such a place exists in New Orleans and I don't know about it?"

"It does and it is the most terrifying, upsetting thing I ever witnessed. Every detail is carried out with the utmost attention to effect. One's anonymity is carefully preserved and a sense of complete protection is achieved. All of it should be frightening but as it is, the only frightening thing about it is the show. It is frightening because it brings out such elemental things in people. Women were sobbing from sheer nervous tension when it was over. One even screamed. I broke out in such a sweat that one would have thought I'd been in a hard game of tennis."

"Would you take me?" His voice was tense and eager.

She thought for a moment. "I don't know. I might be able to arrange it through T'ling."

"I'd consider it a great favor if you would. I don't know when anything has appealed to me like this." He sat back and seemed to relish the thought immensely. "So you found out about it through T'ling?"

"Yes. She thought you were a bad influence and I think her idea was to introduce me to the elements in their rawest form and thus wean me."

"T'ling is disgustingly normal and her reaction was the same. She, nevertheless is a delightful combination of bloods. She has beauty."

"She has something. I dropped her by the Banford Arms tonight."

"Um … you don't say? Who is he?"

"She didn't say. Only that he was known to the Madam and 'worked' there occasionally."

He chuckled. "I've heard of men like him but I've never had the opportunity of meeting one."

Favra got up and dressed. "I'm going home now. I'm so disturbed I know I won't sleep."

"Go ride on the ferry till you get sleepy," he advised. "I find it very restful and soothing to the nerves."

CHAPTER 3
AFFAIR ON A FERRY

FAVRA FOUND herself on the ferry after reacting to Aaron's suggestion without thinking about it. Was he correct in saying that she did not know consciously what her true desires were?

She sat on a plain wooden bench on the top deck thrilling when the whistle boomed in her ear, gasping with consternation when the wind caught her soft dress and blew it to her waist before she could haul it down again. The river had a pungent smell, warm, and flavorful like myriads of cooking smells overlaid with crude oil and garbage. It was a lusty smell that seemed to carry some suggestion of the awful strength of the great stream, a smell that was just what one would expect of a mighty river taking down to the sea the flotsam and waste from half a continent. She stretched her legs before her, trying to get her mind off the pulsing desires of her body, the sullen demand for raw red living, the unvoiced cry for the things it was so marvelously suited to perform. She thought back to her first introduction to sex. It had been on her grandfather's ranch where the mating of animals was something so commonplace that no one else paid it much attention unless it was some unscheduled mixing of strains that any breeder of live stock is careful to avoid. She was fourteen, just beginning to bud, just beginning to fill out from her years of awkward legginess that had often made her cry when alone comparing herself to the ugly duckling. She had been absorbed with things of self for a long time because of her awkwardness and was given to studying herself before her mirror searching for some signs of the birth of the swan. She greeted the first swell of her breasts with glee, and immediately began pestering her mother for certain articles of grown-up apparel. She got them and used them assiduously until it came to such matters as lacquered satin evening dresses with boned fronts. What she got was demure frocks of dotted swiss and organdy with puffed sleeves and modest necklines. Her young aunt, Molly McMullin, who was only two years her senior was the sort of girl who did little to keep her mind from fleshly things, and at the age of fourteen Favra was an avid listener when Molly related some of the juicier details of her dates.

It was bedtime and the girls were lying on their bed without covering, as the night was hot. Molly's body sent splinters of the greenest envy through her niece, nor was she unconscious of the affect of it. She drew in her stomach and made her pointed breasts rise enticingly. "Do you know what Alvin Banter did the other night while I was kissing him?"

"No, what?"

"He ... well ..."

"*No.*"

"He certainly did."

"Did you slap him?"

"No, it was too late."

"And you let him?" Favra's voice was hushed with horror.

Her aunt shrugged. "Well, I guess we have to grow up sometime ... don't you say a word to mama. She's awfully old fashioned."

"Oh ... I wouldn't say anything to *her.*"

"Or anyone?"

"Or anyone ... cross my heart. Is that all he did?"

"No ... not exactly but I didn't let him get very far like Susy Kelliland. She's *terrible.*"

"What does she do?"

"She lets boys—you know—"

She didn't know what Molly meant but since it was only a detail she nodded as though it were old stuff.

At sixteen, which was the minimum dating age in the McMullin family, she and Molly began to double date when she visited for the summer. Remembering that Molly allowed certain liberties with boys, Favra did the same, but with different results. After a ride one night during which her escort had taken certain liberties that left her breathless and frightened but so excited that she could hardly think, they divided so as to afford more privacy and on a rustic seat in a dark corner of the yard Favra soon found that the situation threatened to break its bonds and escape her control.

She managed to catch a second's respite during which time she saw herself as the object of deviltry. She jerked herself erect with such violence that her surprised swain was deposited on the ground and snatching up her lingerie departed with such speed that the frantic boy, all manner of fears ordering him to placate her, could not catch her.

"What," Molly wanted to know, "happened to you and Albert? He seemed frightened to death when he left."

"*He* seemed frightened! What do you think I felt?" She described the occurrence with drama and without much protective coloring.

"Whew," breathed Molly. "You did have a close squeak."

Favra stretched her long legs out before her and inhaled the exciting oily stench of the Father of Waters. Her reflections had done little to ease her mind and she had to fight down the wish that some strong man would come along and ... Resolutely she put the thought aside. Since that terrifying night she had so carefully kept her dating free of all things leading to passion that her college life had been a continuous parade of dating different boys. She was so parsimonious with her kisses that few of them ever managed to satisfy their urge to pet, leaving her eventually or sooner for greener pastures.

Now at the age of twenty-two she felt she had reached the end of her tether. Had it not been for Aaron she doubtless, could have gone along living her life of luxury and ease without becoming involved but his attentions had aroused a fiend within her that he could not satisfy. How, she thought, could I have allowed him, when I would most certainly have balked at the real thing?

On the Algiers side, the big ferry scraped slowly to a landing. Men ran to the side nearest the landing and threw hawsers, making the vessel fast, whereupon it began to disgorge its cargo of passengers and cars. People stood in line waiting to get on and after the last passenger had gone ashore they filed on casually and handed over their tickets to the collector.

The last man aboard caught her eye. He was middle-aged with a fine shock of bristly blond hair, his skin reddened from much exposure. He was big-boned and powerful, his shoulders broad and his bare arms muscular and hard. She breathed quickly and sat back on her bench trying to shake off the thrill the sight of him had initiated. She was relieved to hear the first puff of steam that signaled the departure of the ferry and braced herself for the blast of the whistle. It came and showered her with fine droplets of condensed steam, the sweetish smell of it coming to her nostrils that were highly sensitive tonight. She writhed slightly on the seat biting her bottom lip with vexation and irritation. She was a mass of throbbing nerves, growing more and more restless. She'd go home as soon as she could get off the boat, take a sleeping capsule and try to sleep. She rarely used them but tonight she knew she'd never get to sleep in her present state.

Steps rasped on the companionway and before she had time to move a man sat beside her. It would be the big man that she had seen come aboard. She was certain of it, yet she dared not look, feeling absurdly excited, becoming disgusted with her erratic emotions. She should get up and move ... or something, but that would be unnecessarily offensive. After all, what could happen on a ferry-boat?

He sat quietly at the other end of her bench, then gave a start. "Sorry, ma'm. I didn't know anybody was up here."

"That's all right," she said slowly to retain control of her voice.

"Nice place to sit. A body can get the wind in his hair up here."

"And get showered when the whistle blows," she said with a high pitched giggle.

"Yeah, that's right. Cigarette, ma'm?"

"Yes, if you don't mind."

He extended the pack toward her and moved closer but not frighteningly close. She accepted a cigarette nervously and tapped it on her thumbnail. The man smelled good. He was clean, not long out of a bath, she guessed, because she could get a whiff of masculine soap that had a smell like phenol. He struck a match and extended it toward her, his eyes fixed on her face.

"It is nice here. I couldn't sleep tonight so I tried riding the ferry to get sleepy. I'm wider awake than ever now."

"That happens," he conceded. "Sometimes I work overtime and when I do I get home so tired that I can't sleep. That's bad."

"What do you do to get to sleep?"

"Sometimes I get up and go to the corner and get me a half pint of whiskey. Then I make two drinks out of it and that'll put me to sleep."

"It would me too," she said. "I doubt if I'd wake up, though."

"I don't know. I've known some women that'd drink any man under the table."

"Maybe they were cheating."

"Could be. A man drinks too fast mostly. Women like to sorta stagger along with their drinkin'."

"What's that thing over us?"

"Kind of a roof and a deck combined. They got the life rafts up there and not much else. A little rail to keep curious people from falling overboard."

"I don't see any way to get up there."

"Sure...right there behind you. A ladder. There's a hatch above at the top of the ladder. A kid could move it. Wanter go up?"

"Yes, I'd like to."

"Okay...now put out your hand. There's a little light now. See the ladder?"

Excitement began to dam up inside her as she nodded and walked toward the ladder. Her caution was now so dulled that its small voice could scarcely be heard amid the turmoil of racing blood and tingling nerves. She climbed the ladder with him close behind her...was the heat she felt on her buttocks his breath...was he that close? A shiver shook her.

" 'Smatter, cold?"

"Just a little." She reached the hatch and pushed against it with her right hand. "Maybe a child could move it but I can't. It seems to be stuck."

"Just stand fast. I'll climb up behind you and move it." The heat from his body accentuated by her state of hypersensitivity made her head swim giddily. Again the smell of clean starched khakis, tobacco, and *man*. Her throat felt constricted as she watched him move the obstacle as though it were a piece of cardboard. "Okay, up you go."

She went through the hatch and found herself on a small deck surrounded by a low rail and two ranks of thick gray-painted boards with handholds cut in them. She leaned back against one slanted rank of planks.

"Them things ain't likely to be very clean."

"That's all right. I'm having fun and I won't let the thought spoil it."

"Say, you know...you're all right."

"Thanks ... oh, hell, we're docking."

"Sure. No sooner'n we get here we got to get down."

"I don't. I'm just riding. Do you have to go?"

He was quiet for a moment standing before her, big, rugged, his thick arms hanging easily by his sides. "No'm ... I don't have to go. I'll take another ride with you." His reply had been slow and deliberate, so much so that her stomach seemed to contract with tension, anticipation, and nervousness. He turned and placed his back against the planks the move putting them within touching distance. He dug out his cigarettes again and again she took one. He let the match burn longer this time taking in the slim elegance of her body and the sprouting bounty of her breasts.

Favra felt like screaming. Why wouldn't the boat move? Why was it waiting so long. She had studied his face when he lit her cigarette, its lined hardness, prominent but thin nose, full controlled lips that stayed in her mind's eye when the light went out.

"This is nice," he said quietly. The deference was gone from his voice and he seemed to feel more at ease. "Little windier up here, though ..." The whistle blasted hoarsely hiding them in a warm wet blanket that soon blew away leaving them chilled. She shivered again and sniffled.

"You're likely to catch cold up here."

"No ... *no.*" That wasn't good. Too vehement. Calming herself by force she added. "I rarely take colds."

"I'll stand here to take some of the wind off you."

He stood in front of her, his big body shielding her from the northeast wind, the heat of him coming to her steadily.

"What's your name?"

"Elton Chance ... what's yours?"

"Favra McMullin."

"That Favra part sounds foreign. McMullin is as homey as Hogan's goat."

"I'll bet you're wondering what I'm *really* doing on this boat."

"Nope. I don't wonder into other people's business."

A little silence fell between them and she could tell that he had grown suddenly conscious that he was standing very close to her. Close enough that his breath fanned a tendril of hair at her ear. The ferry was just swinging away from the landing and it had grown relatively dark. Clouds covered the moon except for brief excursions into the open, something for which Favra was intensely thankful. She would have preferred total darkness but partial obscurity was second best. She licked her lips and looked up at him and even in the dark she knew that his eyes were meeting hers. Was he closer or was it fancy... No, his hands have gone on either side of me...

"Favra."

"Yes, Elton?"

"You can stop me anytime you want to."

Her answer was a quick surge toward him, and when his hard hungry lips touched hers there was a momentary blacking out, and only his strong arms encircling her kept her from falling. She regained her strength and strove to keep the sound in her throat from becoming too loud but his arms were bruising her back, his lips were crushing hers, his muscle-ribbed stomach pressed to hers, driving out her breath, and his oaklike chest compressed her breasts till the strap of her brassiere cut into her back. She whimpered incoherently imploring him to crush her more, hurt her, bruise her, but no word could be understood. Her mouth was forced open by a particularly brutal attack and she could taste the saltiness of her own blood from a slight cut on her nether lip. His attentions were transferred to her throat, her neck, the shell-like curvature of her ears.

Her hands clutched his thick hair with such force that she could feel him resisting her but she pulled all the harder. A scream rose to her throat that she choked into a gurgle because his attentions had changed their locale. She arched herself away from the cold planks holding him hard against her, writhing from the waves of rocketing sensation set up by his rough hands. I'll scream ... I know it ... I can't help it ... What's wrong with me ... ? Am I going mad ... ?

"Oh ... Elton ... Elton ... *Elton*." The air was chill against her but it was something that she hardly had the clarity of mind to realize. She clutched him, feeling the rippling muscles of his back and the restrained power of his arms that both held her up and maneuvered her as easily as a child. Then with shocking suddenness she *knew*.

And all her fears were gone, replaced by a wild, soaring joy which made her scream strange words and stranger exhortations in his ear. Her words seemed to force his hands and they slipped from around her and found her eager, caressing her. The sensation plunged her into a taut contraction. She relaxed bonelessly. Favra forced her face against him hard.

His answer was more of a noise than a word as he laid her back on the deck, his tongue driving her into frantic exertion. Hard rigors ran through her and her breath rasped from the force of her breathing.

"Oh, God, Elton ..." He held her easily, restraining her frenzy with gentle but positive strength. Sweat dripped from her face as she drew in long shuddering gasps of air, relaxed against him, so utterly spent that she could not have stood alone. He kissed her with understanding tenderness and held her close till at last she began to approach normalcy.

"Elton, you're ... You're ..." She shook her head and held onto him for a long moment before looking at him again. "You're terribly nice."

"To you," he said huskily, "how could a man be anything else. You're something I never had no dealings with before. You're high class. I was a little scared."

"Oh, no. Why, you were so kind, so gentle, and ..." She shuddered and clutched him again. "I think you're one of the finest gentlemen I ever met."

"Geez … thanks but I ain't got a lot of education, you know."

"They don't get to be gentlemen that way," she said fiercely. "I know."

"Nope. I'll find out later that I dreamed the whole thing. Sorry, but I don't believe you."

He helped her down to the place of their meeting and they sat in silence feeling each other's closeness and not wanting to break the spell till at last the ferry began to approach the New Orleans side again.

Later as they walked out under the street lights he stopped her. "Here, lemme look you over good. I don't believe any such thing happened to me tonight. Fellers like to tell tales like this but it never happens and I know it."

Her smile was misty. "It happened all right and I'm real."

She caught his arm and pulled herself close. "Look at me. Now … right over there is my car. If you don't think I'm real we'll go to my apartment. I think I can convince you."

He grinned showing white uneven teeth. "I'm all for it. You ain't married?"

"No."

"Don't you know better'n to run risks?"

She kissed him with swift impulsive affection. "I think you're perfectly wonderful."

"That'd be fine but for one thing."

"What's that?"

"I'll tell you sometime."

Elton seemed to fill the apartment, bulking larger than he had on the ferry, his head almost reaching the low ceiling. She expected him to feel out of place, embarrassed, ill at ease, but he came in, sauntered to the ivory couch and sat down as though such luxurious items were common to him.

"Shall I make you a drink?"

"Yes, please. Whiskey if you have it."

She went to her little bar and made two drinks, a growing wonder nudging her mind. Why had he seemed so at home in an atmosphere that must be foreign to him? Why had even his speech changed, or had she imagined that? She handed him a drink and sat beside him. "Would it embarrass you if I told you that this was the most wonderful night in my life?"

"Nope. The first one is always very beautiful or very horrible or very dull. More often the first two."

He tasted his drink with a fastidiousness that spoke of a different person than the rough and possibly uncouth man she had originally thought him to be. She finished her drink. "Are you in a hurry?"

"Me … ? No, m'am. I got all night."

"I'm going to bathe. I feel gritty and maybe sooty from the ferry."

"You look like a white fawn just dried off after a hard rainstorm."

"That's nice, but I don't feel that way. I'll be back in a little while."

"If you don't mind me using your bath I'd like to take a quick duck, too. I don't feel as sanitary as I might, after all that smoke and steam blowin' around."

She came back and knelt beside him on the couch. "Of course I don't mind … Elton."

"Thanks," he said huskily pulling her into his lap. His kiss left her so weak that she had to make a determined effort to stand up. She looked at him, her eyes making a blur of his figure, then turned and went into the bedroom, thence to the bath. She disrobed and as in times past surveyed herself critically in the mirror. A stab of luxurious sensation struck her, making a slight chill twit her skin. She turned to her shower and ten minutes later stepped into a white silk robe and went back into the living room. "It's all yours, Elton."

He stood and took her in his arms, again his hard lips forcing her head back and his arms making her ribs crack from the force of his embrace.

He released her and stepped back, taking in the pliant wonder of her body under its thin clinging covering. She watched him trance-like through eyes that had darkened with a passion that muttered like thunder in the distance, her lips parted and her breath ragged.

"Hurry back, Elton."

She listened to his noisy ablutions and when the running water ceased to hiss she got up and walked into the bedroom. He stood in the open door his back to her, wreathed in cabled muscle, a deep trench down his back, his shoulders seeming broader than ever. He finished drying, stood before the mirror, made a face at himself, draped his middle with the towel and came into the bedroom. He stopped when he saw her standing slim and straight by the bed looking at him fixedly, her eyes liquid and soft, her lips damp.

"You said I wasn't real." She shrugged. "What do you think now?"

For a long moment he stood transfixed with the wonder of her standing there before him, palpitant, a translucent pearl.

"Lordy," he muttered thickly. "I believe it less than before. It can't be."

With a sob she flung herself into his arms, urging herself to every line of his body, her mouth begging silently. Again his lips bruised hers with the force of his kiss, the javelin of her tongue meeting, embracing his. A kind of transcendental madness possessed her, a madness that took her out of the sphere of mere humanity, placed her in an exalted plane where colors were sharp and brilliant, strange music sounded as clear as a bell note on a frosty morning. From a mere earthly body she became a glowing goddess of fantastic beauty, a nymph worshiping at the altar of ecstatic splendor, a naiad not of the mean medium of flesh,

48

blood and bone but something from a fable, all rhythm, glowing without, a reflection of the fires within like a luminous tube of ivory with the flexibility of spring steel and the tireless strength of Aphrodite.

Dawn came and inserted an apologetic finger of light into the room. She still retained him in her embrace even in a death-like sleep, her hair spread on the pillow like a fan of gold. The sun was hard at work painting the spire of the Cathedral when they sat across her small breakfast table and drank coffee. "I can cook some breakfast, Elton."

"No, I've stayed too long—I'll have to hurry." He stood up and when she stood beside him he bent and kissed her gently on the lips without passion, without roughness, but with infinite affection. The touch and his attitude made a lump come to her throat. "When … I mean, shall I see you again?"

He shrugged. "Who can say? We might meet on the ferry again. Remember last night when I told you that your idea that I was wonderful was all right but for one thing?"

"Yes. I meant to ask you about that."

His eyes were level and a deep intense blue. "I'm a married man, Favra. A happily married man with four daughters and twin sons. All grown or nearly so. Goodbye." He kissed her again and turning, walked out of the kitchen. He was halfway down the steps to the street before she regained command over her stricken limbs and dashed after him.

"Elton … Elton …" she ran down the steps careless of house coat that had divided leaving her naked from the waist down. She threw herself sobbing into his arms. "You can't leave me like this, you can't … you can't …"

He held her close and stroked her head. "How else can I leave you, my dear? You wouldn't want me to lie to you, would you? Wouldn't you rather know now than later when I might become a habit?"

"No … no … no …" She gulped noisily gripping him with despairing strength. "Yes, I suppose so … Oh, I don't know anything … Tell me how I should feel … tell me what to do."

"Right now you'll go back into your house. In the future you'll act like any intelligent girl would. You'll find other interests. Do you know how old I am, Favra?"

"N-no."

"Forty-five and if you're a day over twenty-five I don't know it. I have two sons who are twenty-eight. I was a father at the age of seventeen."

She tossed her head and compressed her lips. "I'm sorry. I forgot myself for a moment. Goodbye."

She turned and started dispiritedly up the stairs. Elton turned abruptly on his heel and walked away realizing that she had stopped halfway to the door and was watching him.

CHAPTER 4
SOME TRUTHS ABOUT LOVE

"IF ALL your lessons are as easy as the first, my dear, you're off to a good start."

"Oh...Alice, you frightened me. Please come in. I need someone to talk to. I'll make more coffee."

She came down the steps and assisted the old woman to the door which she opened then closed and locked after they were inside.

"I don't want to see anyone," she said, a catch in her voice. "Alice, how much did you see...hear?"

"I saw everything. I heard everything. He told you in the house and it was such a shock that you couldn't move for a moment and then you came running after him."

"How could you know that?"

Alice shrugged and bared her silver head shaking the cape down to the nape of her neck.

"It was obvious enough, and it happens often enough. Was he wonderful?"

Favra sank down on the couch and sobbed wretchedly. "No words can explain how wonderful he was...it was." She raised her head and whispered. "All night...all night he was mine and now he's gone." She sank down and began to cry again. Alice rapped her sharply across the ankles with her cane. It hurt and made the girl sit up in perplexity.

"Now," said the old woman her voice ringing in a manner Favra had never heard. "That is quite enough. You've wallowed in heaven, now in hell. Snap out of it and live on earth with the rest of us for awhile. There'll be other trips, believe me … to both places. You invited me in for coffee."

"Yes, of course, come on back in the kitchen." Alice was another person she couldn't make out. The suddenness with which she had changed from an ancient old witch into a commanding woman whose voice rang with authority was no less amazing than the many-sided Elton she had been afraid to question. Her ankle ached from the authority of the stick too, a matter for further thought. She had been struck, not brutally but sharply, hard enough to send a stab of pain up her legs. She made coffee and they sat at the table drinking. "What did you mean by saying I had learned an easy lesson? I can't see the easy part."

Alice selected a cheroot from the folds of her black garment and applied a match to it.

"To begin with, you managed to have your first experience with a man whose status, marital, and otherwise, is such that you are prevented from making a fool of yourself, a state which is ripe for the plucking at the moment. It is hard to believe that any man could have been so immensely wise and thoughtful that he could have made your first night out, so to speak, such a success. How sublimely lucky you are there. No one save someone like myself, whose initial experience made love more bitter than sweet for so many years, is really qualified to tell you this. Your first and to the many your toughest obstacle is past. From now on you have only to equal this."

"How can you say that?" cried Favra bitterly. "How can it possibly be equaled?"

"They are never duplicated really, my dear," said Alice gently, "only equaled more or less. You'll see …"

Favra ran her fingers through her hair pulling it cruelly. Her body ached and each little separate pain was as precious to her as any possession she had.

"Where's the Professor this morning?" she asked to make conversation.

"He ate very early and left before we could catch him there."

Favra raised her eyebrows. "But why on earth?"

"I think he's short of cash."

"That's pitiful. One can see that he tries hard to make ends meet and still keep up appearances. Isn't there something we can do?"

Alice tapped a length of ash into her saucer. "I have a small income that though generally prompt is late this month."

"I didn't really mean it like that. Naturally, I'd do it. Oh hell, I have all kinds of money, Alice. It's time I did something worthwhile with it." A thought struck her with stinging force. Alice was short and the Professor was short at the same time of the month. It was a stupid thought, she told herself, but what if she were right? She lowered her eyes to meet those of the old woman. As she looked at her she could recall any number of things ... "Alice, look me in the eyes, now, what has the Professor's embarrassment to do with your late dividend?"

Alice turned pink but retained her composure. "I have underestimated you," she said quietly.

Tears came to Favra's eyes. "I think that's about the most wonderful thing I ever heard."

"To you it seems wonderful. To me it is a must. I'll die some day but I couldn't live knowing that he was starving or in dire want. I suppose I should tell you the story because I know you won't tell him and you do have a kind heart."

"Please tell me."

"The man whom you know as the Professor is really a member of one of New Orleans' most illustrious families. They are wealthy and proud. That's where he gets his pride. There was a time when he was one of the City's most open-handed and dashing playboys. I was a neighbor, my family rather, and it was inevitable sooner or later that we should meet. I was rather dashing myself for those days and a great deal more dashing than was public knowledge. I had had one disastrous affair, one that sent me crazily hunting for what I had missed. There were several more over a period of years and finally I met *him*. We had similar tastes, a sneer and a snapped finger for codes and such things. We were well met, and for some time, a year or more, we together made the brightest light in town. Then it happened. I paid the supreme penalty for freedom in love and he, bless him, wanted to do the right thing. His family wouldn't hear of it and packed him off to Rio. You can imagine how my family felt then and they haven't spoken to me since, those who are left."

"What of the child?" Favra was tense.

"It died at birth, which I suppose was a blessing, because my family's fortunes declined, it seemed, from the date of my trouble. Most of them are dead and those who are still living think I'm dead. It is better that way."

"But they … don't they run into you down here?"

"Oh, I see some of them occasionally, the younger ones, grand nieces and nephews and the like but they don't know me. You see, I'm not exactly what I once was."

"But what about the Professor?"

"He came back from South America and announced his decision to marry me in the face of all objection so he was cut loose. It was one of those silly things where the family goes into mourning and there is everything but a notice in the obituary column. He is declared dead by the family."

"But he didn't marry you."

"No, because I disappeared. I didn't want him to lose everything because I knew how dear to him good living and money were. I didn't come back to New Orleans until many years later. I had a little income as I told you from some stocks my mother left me but that was all so I took to drink; I went down rapidly, lost my pride and although I have never begged … this might amuse you, the tiny distinction I make … I seem to be an object of pity which makes people want to give me money. It was easy and it helped buy whiskey so I made myself as pitiable as possible." She touched the cheroot to the remnants of coffee and laid it carefully on the saucer.

"I saw him one day at the French Market and the very first time he gallantly invited me to have breakfast with him. That marked the end of my drinking … and he has never recognized me. When I found out that he was living in a hovel, existing on a paltry little income from some carelessly invested windfall, race-track winnings probaably, I suffered more, I think, than when I had to leave him."

"And you began to divide your income with him anonymously," Favra's voice was rich with compassion.

Alice nodded listlessly. "It isn't much that I can spare him but it helps buy little things and he is at least living in a comfortable room now."

"Isn't there something he can do? Didn't he teach once?"

"It is a bit of romantic fiction which he likes to keep alive. He always spoke very precisely and that earned him the name of Professor. I think he painted at one period in his life but I don't think he was very good."

"Tragedies like that always make me ill."

Alice smiled. " 'Tis an ill wind … You see, my dear, worse things can happen than what you experienced this morning."

"I'm ashamed. I'm afraid I've been very selfish."

"Have a care now." Her voice was sharp with command again. "Don't let our troubles become yours."

"Alice, why don't you tell him who you are?"

"I don't know. I suppose I want him to remember me as I was. That, I guess, is the remnant of pride I have left."

"I'm going to get personal. How much do you give him and how is it given?"

"I send him a letter enclosing cash anonymously. I give him ten dollars once a month."

Favra's vision blurred. She had paid more than that for a piece of costume jewelry, worn it once and given it to T'ling.

"Will you do something for me?"

The old woman nodded, her eyes questioning.

"See me once a month and instead of ten I'll give you fifty. I won't miss it and he'll be able to get some new linen and clothes. I think it'll be a great boost for his ego. Keep your ten and please, please let me know if I can ever do anything for you. Why don't you let me get some decent clothes for you … a better place to live .. ?"

"No, dear, I can't let you do that. For him, yes, but not for me. What would I do with them? In better clothes he might recognize me. I see him nearly every day, and I am of some use to him. I'd rather it stayed that way. Now I must leave and become a tottering old woman for the tourists to pity. I have a living to make."

Favra gave her a quick squeeze that revealed a surprise. Instead of a spare shrinking bag of bones she caught a well fleshed solid arm and shoulder She sprang back and gazed accusingly at her. "Alice, how old are you?"

She stood erect, her head back and her eyes flashing. "I've told you everything else and I am at your mercy. I might as well tell you all. I am fifty years old."

For a moment Favra could only stare open-mouthed, wondering.

"People are not hard to deceive. Before you touched me you would have thought I could not possibly have weighed a hundred pounds, wouldn't you?"

"I would have staked my life that you wouldn't weigh that much."

"So with others. This shapeless garment, the hood over white hair with a tendril or two peeping out, the cane, the bent shambling gait. I have become quite good at makeup, too. Penciled wrinkles are quite convincing if they are applied properly and if others are already conditioned to expecting them."

"Wait a moment. I think I have enough in my purse." She came back immediately with three bills. "Get these to him today, Alice. I wouldn't want you to miss a single breakfast with him."

Alice took the money and turned it over before hiding it in the recesses of her clothes. "And there is one more thing I'd like to ask of you."

"Just ask it."

"Will you remove your housecoat?"

She was taken aback somewhat but nevertheless she complied and stood nude before the older woman. For a long moment she stared at the girl almost hypnotically, then nodded with manifest satisfaction. "I wanted another look at myself when I was that age ... but I was never that lovely. Thank you, my dear, and now I'll leave you."

Favra put her coat back on and went to her bedroom to dress. She was still sleepy, but she had to go somewhere, do something.

T'ling came in and before she could rearrange the bed the girl had seen it. Her face was glowing with joy. "It worked, Miss Favra ... it worked."

"Yes, you minx, it worked and now I'm beaten to bits. I found the most wonderful man in the world and lost him the same night." Her grief gripped her again and she slid down on her bed and T'ling whose heart was very tender sank to a footstool. "Gee ... I'm sorry, Miss Favra."

She sat up angrily and tossed her heavy hair. "I'm being weak and silly again. It's not your fault, T'ling. If I'm to play this hand I've dealt myself I can't whine every time a card falls wrong. I'm hungry. Will you scramble a couple of eggs for me?"

The girl leaped up anxious to do something. "Yes, ma'm, I'll be glad to, and I'll make some fresh coffee."

"Fine. I need something, so I'll start with food."

She slipped into blue shorts and a white T-shirt, brushed her hair till it shone like polished metal and went into the living room to wait till T'ling called her to breakfast. She stopped short as she went through the door then continued till she reached the couch and sat beside Aaron.

"You startled me."

"I noticed. I also seem to have heard lamentations and recriminations from behind yon door. Did the ferry ride turn out badly?"

"Terribly...in a sense. How did you know I went ferry riding?"

"It is obvious to observing eyes, hoofprints all over the place and a subtle difference in you."

"What do you mean, hoof prints?"

"Made by the stallion I so confidently predicted would gallop into your life."

She compressed her lips. "All right, I'll admit he was here but I want to know how you knew it?"

"I knew it before I found evidence. I seem to sense things like that. Concretely speaking, I never knew you to smoke anything but Luckies. There is a Camel in the ash tray that had been thoroughly tamped and the loose paper bitten off. I don't think your habits have changed that much."

"Very well. I found him on the ferry."

"How utterly romantic. Was he nice?"

"The nicest man I ever met and dammit I'll have none of your sarcasm...please, I am not up to it."

He studied her keenly. "Your attitude and lamentations of a while ago can mean but one thing. The bubble burst before it was fully blown."

"You're correct again if it affords you any pleasure."

"Not pleasure necessarily, just entertainment in seeing you suffer from growing pains. Maybe you are just twenty-two after all."

"If anyone ever thought of me as a barnacled sophisticate they read it into me. I never claimed to be."

"I suppose you're right. Yet you associate easily with the crowd save for certain intervals of truculence for which you may be forgiven … by the way, it has been reliably reported that about one more foot pound of energy, no pun mind you, and you would have made an eternal whisperer of Ecco. I hear his gullet was effectually pulverized but they think it possible to make him some sort of noise box through which he may make known simple wishes."

"I'm sorry," she said, "if I injured him permanently but I'm not sorry I kicked him. The idea of letting that repellent vulture have me makes me retch."

"And I also. I take it that the stallion made no such impression."

"He was the most wonderful man I ever met."

"Why the long face then?"

"Because he is married and unless I barge into him some place, as I did last night, I will never see him again. Evidently he wasn't as impressed as I was."

"That is deliberate flagellation. If the man has responsibilities then you can hardly expect him to throw them over the side just because he met you."

"I have money and I could give him everything … speaking in terms of cash, I could grant his every wish."

His eyes narrowed. "Describe this paragon to me. I'm curious."

T'ling came in, gave Aaron a quick stony look and announced breakfast.

"Will you join me? I'm going to have a bite."

"Some coffee, perhaps. I've eaten. I'll go back and you can describe this man to me while you eat."

She described him well without sparing herself in the description and the refreshed memory all but destroyed her appetite.

He sipped his coffee delicately for a moment before answering. "Several things do not seem to hang together."

"What?"

"First you say he is a common ordinary laborer, dresses and talks like one, yet is gentle, kind, thoughtful, a … er, master, we might say. Mind you, I'm not a social snob, only an intellectual one, and I will admit without contest that there are probably laborers who are all that but it is not the common picture of a laborer. Moreover, he was clean, another thing that sits uneasily with the picture as it stands. I'll admit clean laborers too, without batting an eye, I would even insist on them but … drat it, this man has too many things he has no business having. Lastly, he attracted you. Granting every other question I brought up as being false and ill considered, I still cannot see you being attracted to a horny-handed toiler with tools. Debutantes fall in love with chauffeurs in lesser numbers than certain dull novelists would have us believe."

Favra banged her toast down on the plate. "I felt the very same way. I didn't actually put my finger on points like you, but I *felt* it. Something … I don't know, but something made me feel … Oh, yes. How many horny-handed toilers as you call them, could come into my living room and be perfectly at home. Wouldn't you expect them to feel clumsy, out of place?"

"Of course … wondering if on some off chance they hadn't tracked manure on your Chinese rug."

"Yes, something like that, but not Elton. He came in, glanced at my place with an appreciative eye, then accepted it as gracefully as you."

"And his name is Elton …"

"Oh," she interrupted. "When he got here he seemed to have to force his laborer's speech which came so naturally on the ferry that I was surprised when he dropped it."

"Aha … the conditioned reflex again. In a lady's quarters he began to speak like a gentleman."

"Not entirely but there was a trend in that direction. He seemed to have to make an effort to speak like a worker."

Aaron lighted a cigarette and inhaled deeply. "Elton … the name rings a bell, faintly. No, I take it back. I went to school with a boy whose last name was Elton. What was the man's full name?"

"Elton Chance."

"Elton Chance …" His white even teeth showed as his lips curved in a slow smile. "Favra, I don't know what you'd do without me."

"What do you mean?"

"Do you have a *Times Picayune* of last Sunday?"

"I think so. We save them from week to week and a boy picks them up. T'ling …"

"Yes'm."

"Will you see if last Sunday's paper is still in the closet … what section, Aaron?"

"Financial and real estate."

"Aaron, what is this?"

"Another lesson in your education … ah, here we are." He took the paper from T'ling and searched for a moment. "Here we are. Read here about this construction company that is building a lot of dock space and repair yards for the Navy around Algiers and Gretna."

She read in silence then put the paper down her eyes soft and dreamy. "Why, the man is probably a millionaire."

"I think you're putting it altogether too mildly. The man is undoubtedly a millionaire and probably several times a millionaire. In case you haven't heard of the family, and I can see that you haven't, I'll brief you. They are a long line of ship builders, construction men, and Navy greats. There were two of the brothers in the Pacific during the last war. Admiral Chance fought gallantly, leading a destroyer squadron under Halsey and Mitscher.

The other is in submarines, Lieutenant Commander Bannerman Chance. Another operates the biggest shipbuilding concern on the Mississippi coast. Elton is in construction of all sorts. His company has built causeways, skyscrapers, docks and about anything else you can mention. One of his peculiarities is dressing shabbily and mixing freely with his men. They adore him. It has been said that he can thrash or outdrink any man who ever worked for him."

"I can believe that," she breathed. "Muscles, arms like posts, legs like piling. And he was such a gentleman…" Her eyes filled quickly and she turned her head away.

"Are you ashamed of tears?" he asked gently.

"I'm ashamed of the weakness that makes me shed them."

"All sensitive people are weak, then. If there were no sensitive people there would be no beauty because beauty is only reflection in the human."

"I'm afraid I'm not equal to optimistic philosophy."

"I accept the brand but might it not be true as well?"

"Maybe…I don't know. I don't know anything, what I'm going to do…nothing."

"Allow me to suggest that we take a trip to the place you mentioned at my house last night. That at least should get your mind off your troubles."

"That very thing seemed to be the start of my troubles." She looked cautiously about for T'ling but the buzz of the vacuum cleaner made speech safe. "T'ling is sad because she feels responsible for my present state. I don't want her to hear me."

"When will you take me?" he persisted.

"I think they are put on three times a week. I'll ask T'ling and get her to request that you be allowed to attend. It'll cost you twenty-five dollars."

"That is a pittance if it's all you say."

"You'll see for yourself."

"By the way," he said as he was leaving. "Ecco isn't that badly hurt. I was just trying to see how you'd react. He'll be all right."

"I'm afraid I can't whip up much sorrow for Ecco. The very thought of him nauseates me."

"No more than he would any person of taste," he said. "Give me a ring."

He was gone and Favra was at a loss to know what to do, so she sat and gave herself over to dark morbid thoughts.

CHAPTER 5
THE BEAUTIES OF TENNIS

DURING THE following two weeks Favra stayed home, went for short walks, had breakfast with Alice and the Professor, and brooded all the while. Aaron tried to comfort her or sting her out of this state but she sat quietly, looking vacantly through him or out of the window hardly hearing anything he said.

Alice and the Professor did their best to cheer her up, hovered over her at breakfast, suggested this and that pasttime till at last Alice hit upon the answer … so she said, "I think you should exercise. Get so weary that you can hardly put one foot in front of the other. Do you have any hobbies, sports?"

"I like tennis," said Favra listlessly as she picked at her hot doughnut.

"Then play tennis. Do it every day and play like you never did before. You'll sleep better and at least it'll be something to do."

Back at her apartment she went to a closet, pulled forth racket and shoes, put on the latter and went in search of T'ling.

"I wish you would contact the Madam and ask her if I can bring a very close personal friend to her next performance. I should have asked you before now."

"Mr. Festival?"

"Yes."

T'ling's eyes narrowed. "Yes'm, I'll ask her."

"Thank you. I'm going to City Park to play tennis. I'll be back about two and I'll take lunch then."

"Yes'm."

At the club she searched for some girl with whom she might have several fast sets of tennis. Ordinarily there were several girls on the loose also searching for partners but today it was half an hour before she found an opponent. A young girl was striding in from the street with racket swinging in her hand. She looked her over for possible court excellence and found that she was looking at a very delightful female animal. She was not quite as tall as Favra but she had long strong legs, deeply tanned, good full hips that were at the same time trim and smooth. Her waist was very small seeming to roll with a rather seductive motion as she walked. Utter freedom, Favra thought. Not a single tight spot in her entire body. Young, healthy and strong. She can probably whip over a nasty serve. The girl came closer and Favra noticed the firm motion of her full breasts against the thin fabric of her T-shirt, the excellent quality of her skin and the wholesomeness of her face that was clean-cut, handsome and distinctive, having an aura of delicacy and fineness.

"I beg your pardon, but I'm looking for a tennis partner. Do you have an engagement?"

The girl gave her a flashing smile. "No, I don't. I came down hoping for just you. I'm Arden Drake."

"My name's Favra McMullin. I'd be glad to do my poor best."

"I'll bet you're kidding. With that height and those long legs you'll probably beat the ears off me."

Arden opened her can of balls, and for thirty minutes, they pinged easily, neither of them exerting much strength.

"I'm ready if you are," called Arden scooping up two of the balls.

"Let's go then," replied Favra scooping up the third ball. "You serve."

"No, you."

"We'll rally for it."

They rallied for serve and Favra won by smacking a kill shot dead in the center of Arden's stomach as she rushed the net.

"Wow," she complained rubbing the spot gingerly. "I see I've taken my life in my hands."

"Sorry. I didn't mean to hit you."

The flashing smile came again. "Oh, I was just kidding. I should have gotten out of the way."

The end of the first set, however, told a different story with Arden winning it handily at six-four. They got a drink of water, returned to the court and Favra went to work with deadly intent. Her service fairly began to smoke as it skimmed the net and her backhand was less a stroke and more of a smash. Her volley became deadly as she began to rush the net and on a back line exchange she increased her power till at last the ball struck the top of the net with such force that it bounded high and went over the backstop.

"Say," panted Arden as she chased the ball. "I didn't really mean it. I take it all back."

Favra smiled as she rested her back against the backstop wire and waited till the girl retrieved the ball. They started and Favra went on the offensive again, steadily increasing her speed, cutting alley lines to a matter of inches, smashing Arden off balance then cross-courting. The set ended six-two and they rested.

They were seated on the grass letting the sun treat their legs while they treated their hot stomachs to Cokes. "Sorry, but I'm bushed and if I play another set I'll wind up at home in bed."

"Oh, gosh," protested Favra. "Don't even mention another set … well, I'll be … Do my eyes deceive me or is that Linda DeForest with the golf bag?"

"Your eyes are all right. That's Linda all right and she's sporting the tag end of the most gorgeous shiner you ever saw. She claims some chippy put in on her in a French Quarter brawl. Just what she was doing in company with a chippy she didn't say."

"Well, well. What do you know? At any rate I can give you the name of the chippy."

"You can … who?"

"I have it on the most impeccable authority that her name was Favra McMullin."

Arden let go a little shriek. "Oh … *no!*" Then she chuckled delightedly. "You know after seeing you in action that last set I'd say you could swing a good one. Her shiner proves it. Tell me about it."

She hesitated for a moment and Arden put a shapely hand on hers.

"It's all right if you don't want to. If it's personal business, I mean."

"Oh, that's all right. It is a pretty sordid tale …"

"Goody, goody … give."

She told the story with characteristic directness, and Arden listened with such avidity that she noticed it. She finished her story and said, "Don't tell me you're one of these people in New Orleans who are starved for a taste of their own wickedness." Arden's face clouded.

"I suppose I am. I'm not very happy."

"Why?"

The girl sighed with a gustiness that indicated the complexity of her unhappiness. "There must easily be a million things. Father, mother, brother, father, mother, and brother. Six main reasons that multiply themselves like a downhill snowball. It seems that I'm just too divine to walk on the earth like ordinary people. I'm watched and every effort is made to suggest me into sickness, all sorts of revolting vitaminized muck is shoved at me, my boy friends are chosen, that's my brother's department, and of all the limp numbers he can dig up … you simply don't know."

"I'm a good guesser," said Favra grimly. "What would they say if you dated a football player?"

"I did…I did, and they nearly fainted. They worked in relays telling me what a terrible thing I had done to the family escutcheon."

"Oh, God, don't tell me you're one of those poor creatures."

"I am one of those poor creatures and it's killing me."

"You're looking at your twin sister, honey, the difference being that I took off like a ruptured duck and here I am in the American Paris living as I please…correction, as my inner self lets me. I've been gaining the upper hand lately."

"Tell me about it."

"Oh, there's nothing much to tell. Grandfather had money, father didn't do badly but he made a bad plunge and got nicked for his roll and he died of a heart attack. Mother died and left me with my great uncle Dan who lived only about a year leaving me his pile which was nothing to sneeze at. I lived in Dallas and loved it except that this cousin and that began to get in my hair and curtail my operations, holding a totally spurious background over my head that was disinterred *after* the money came. I attended S.M.U. and I came to New Orleans to a Sugar Bowl game one New Year's and I was sold. I could hardly wait to get back and pull up my stakes. I quit the university a junior and I've never regretted it. The Quarter is sordid, evil, smelly, sinful, beautiful, exciting, and totally intriguing. I may travel but I'll always come back." She glanced at Arden and was shocked to see tears in the girl's eyes. "What's the matter, dear?"

"Oh, it *kills* me to see someone who has guts and snap and verve when I don't have any."

"Need any help?"

"What sort of help?"

Favra shook her head smiling. "Oh no. You don't need help—you want to be carried and I'm not a tote mule. Put out some effort and I'll sweat blood for you. You figure it out, tell me what you intend to do and I'll pitch in and help. I won't carry you."

Arden stood up. "Will you come home with me and have lunch?"

"Certainly, I'd love to. I'll call my maid and tell her I won't be home."

Favra was offended first by the Drake home which might have caused quite a stir in the early nineteen hundreds but was now only a bespooled, begingerbreaded dust catcher with multicolored windows, turrets and gables in a tremendous senseless tumble. The second offense came from Leslie, the brother, whose nose was thin, high-bridged, and was not intended as a sound board for speech, the use to which he put it second to breathing, which he did noisily. He was as thin as his nose and in peering through his glasses he managed a sort of reptilian projection that made Favra's blood run cold. He shook hands so loosely that she couldn't help pouring the power on the flaccid paw and had the satisfaction of seeing him wince. Her long smooth legs claimed his attention from then on as long as they sat in the living room and bandied inanities. The effect of his fishy eyes made her shudder and when Arden suggested that they wash up, she was relieved.

"What do you think of Leslie, dear?"

"I think Leslie's absorption in matters moral extends to you alone. He in short is a wolf, optically, at least."

"I think you're mistaken there. He may ogle you but there isn't a pass in him."

"You wouldn't like to make a bet on it, would you?"

"I would and if you win it I'll kiss you ... no, I could do something far better, such as buying you a dozen nylons or something as lagniappe ... if I could see it."

Favra laughed. "I hate to be assertive but I think I could make him drool like a starved pig watching a tub of slop."

They showered and went downstairs again with Favra wearing a pair of Arden's dark blue slacks.

"From what you've told me about your family I feel indecent even in slacks."

"You live in the French Quarter. It couldn't be any worse."

At lunch she met Mr. and Mrs. Drake. The father was an aging counterpart of the son while the mother might have looked like her daughter at the same age. She was the sweet old lady type but before long she saw that it was another case of mistaken identity.

"Arden is not very healthy, Miss McMullin. We hardly expected her to reach maturity."

Favra smiled and made a polite face. Small wonder, she thought, if their board was like this every day, raw carrots, sliced raw beets, endive salad with lemon juice and salt, no pepper or dressing, rye toast, orange juice and milk.

"She needs vitamins and absolutely refuses to take them."

"I should say," offered Favra cautiously, "that there are a good many vitamins in this food."

"No one can *eat* enough vitamins, my dear. Supplementary dosage is always needed."

"One would never have known that she was such a sickly thing to see her play tennis." She couldn't resist this little dig.

"Tennis," snorted Leslie contemptuously. "She plays an atrocious game of tennis."

"Leslie," explained Arden acidly, "was singles champion of the Delta Sigs once."

"Twice," corrected Leslie. "I was also a member of the Tulane Varsity, too."

"Win any championships?" Favra asked brightly.

He colored faintly. "No..."

"If you're better than Arden maybe you and I should get together sometime." She made a solemn vow to get this string bean on the courts and trounce him thoroughly.

"Why... that would be a pleasure. Of course, I wouldn't play my best game so as to make it interesting for you but I could give you a better game than Arden who being sickly, tires easily."

"It was not noticeable this afternoon," she said.

"Seeing and experiencing is one thing," commented Mr. Drake in his rusty voice. "Critical observation is quite another."

"I'm sure Miss McMullin is not interested in the bromides of science, Father," said Leslie leaping gallantly to her rescue.

"You are so perceptive, Leslie," she said demurely.

"He springs from a long line of perceptive forebears," the father informed her. At this bit of gratuitous information she almost laughed.

"Where do you live, my dear?" asked Mrs. Drake, containing her curiosity as long as she could.

"Pirate's Alley."

A quick dense hush fell upon the room.

"Um...did you say Pirate's Alley?" asked Mr. Drake presently.

"Yes. I have an apartment there. I'm doing research for a novel. Dr. Christopher Allengood...you have heard of him possibly, a physicist at the University of Texas. He recommended the locale and I got my apartment through the efforts of...now let me see...a good friend of Dr. Allengood here at Tulane. Oh, yes, Dr. Obermire."

The weight of this crushing announcement drove the silence into deeper hues. Anyone even remotely concerned with the sciences who had not heard of Allengood and Obermire were, to be as charitable as possible, idiots.

Mr. Drake leaned forward. "And you're a friend of Dr. Allengood?"

"He married an aunt on my mother's side."

"Well...and you know Dr. Obermire?"

"Not very well. I've been to his house to dinner. When I first came he was very nice to me."

For some five minutes all energy seemed to be concentrated upon eating but Favra could tell that wheels were grinding painfully. That she had not told the entire truth was a matter which she shrugged off. *If this is what it takes to show these people then I've shown them.* She glowed at the apparent success, so much in fact that she added to it a little.

"Eric Savarney, the mathematician … you know the one who …"

"Of course, of course," said Mr. Drake eagerly. "What about him?"

She shrugged lightly as though it were nothing. "He was at my apartment … a little party I had the other night and he was positively enthralled with the Quarter. As you know he's something of a traveler." *If they knew it they were better informed than she.*

"Yes, yes." The father was eager.

"Well, he said that it was without a doubt one of the truly unique places in the new world, that its sophistication and cosmopolitan atmosphere were unequaled in the United States. You see, I quit school to take up writing and it was his opinion that I had chosen the perfect spot for gathering material."

"I do declare," breathed Mrs. Drake immensely impressed. "I suppose we only think of the French Quarter as a den of iniquity."

"Iniquity, Mrs. Drake, impresses only iniquitous people."

Not even Mrs. Drake whose skin she had decided needed a little thinning could take that bomb without flinching. She blushed and crunched a sliver of carrot. "But what about the young and easily led?"

"Naturally, if one drinks one must inevitably expect to become inebriated unless temperance is observed. Let us say that in the Quarter, true individual expression is possible. No one says nay and no one says yea in the face of a determined course."

"I'm afraid I had quite a different opinion of it," she said faintly.

Smiling sweetly to remove some of the sting, Favra said, "Harking back to Mr. Drake's pronouncement, the one that opened his conversation, we might draw something of a parallel, between people who see but do not observe and those who dog-matize without ever having seen."

Mr. Drake's thin face split in a slow smile revealing several yellow teeth. "I am moved to retract the implication contained in my remark. I find that a ready wit is not necessarily the exclusive province of the scientific mind. However, association with such brilliant men probably had something to do with the nurture of your own intellect."

With lunch over the girls again went upstairs, Leslie watch-ing every step Favra took with avid eyes. Arden slammed the door and hugged her. "Darling, you were marvelous... but why all the championing of the Quarter? So mother wouldn't think you iniquitous?"

Favra squeezed her affectionately. "You haven't guessed?"

Arden's brows knitted thoughtfully. "No, did you have some special reason?"

"I did. You're coming to some of my parties."

She let out a little scream of pure joy. "Oh, you... Favra, I love you."

"Do you know what else I'm going to do?"

"No, what?"

"I'm going to take your brother out on the tennis court and I'm going to beat him to a pulp."

"Do you think you can? He's pretty good."

"He'd better be when I get him. I'm not too bad myself when I want to be."

"I know that all right," said Arden laughing. "In that second set I felt like a novice."

"You did fine but when I get Leslie out there I'm going to be playing over my head. I do when I have to."

"Did you really have Eric Savarney at your place?"

"My dear, I never saw the man in my life. I saw in the paper where he was passing through, had dinner at Antoine's and was on his way to South America; and I couldn't write a book if my life depended on it."

"You are … my God, if I had your nerve and imagination! What about the other two?"

"They were bona fide. Allengood is my uncle and Obermire did several favors for me because he knew Allengood. I used them because I could see that your father was interested in science."

"You certainly did a magnificent job and your not so subtle remarks about anyone who thought the Quarter was a den and that no one lived there but trollops and peculiars was a touch of genius. Mother has a horror of being thought provincial and naive."

"And she is both, pathologically."

"Do you think she'll let me come?"

"I'm sure of it. I'll come get you in my car, having called you previously. Don't be ready, but be everything but. Now I must go. I've a lot to do this afternoon."

"Please don't be too long … inviting me, I mean. You have no idea …"

"I certainly do. I had lunch here, remember."

The girl's eyes filled with tears. "I'm so glad I met you. I haven't felt this happy in years."

Favra eyed her in silence for a moment. "You know, I like you. I don't often like women and this meeting occurred so casually, accidentally. By and large, women bore me to distraction."

In the living room Leslie leaped to his feet and escorted her to the door. "We have enjoyed your visit immensely, Miss McMullin. Will you come again soon?"

"Certainly, if you wish, Leslie. Remember, you promised to polish up my tennis game."

"I'd like that."

"Good, we'll play soon." She got in her car and drove home, realizing for the first time that her own troubles had become immersed in those of another to such an extent that she had scarcely noticed them for hours.

"Maybe that's the way it should be done," she soliloquized. "Alice had an idea anyhow."

When she arrived at her apartment T'ling was just leaving. "The Madam says that if you'll vouch personally for Mr. Festival it'll be all right, and you know something?"

"What's that?"

"I told her about him and I think he interested her. She sure sounded like it."

"You mean she's never run into his sort?"

"I don't see how that could be because I thought she knew all about people like him but she sure did sound interested."

"Maybe it's because very few men like him ever *want* women."

"Yes'm, maybe that's it."

"Do you want to go with us?"

"No, ma'm," T'ling giggled. "I've got a date."

"Same place?"

She giggled again and averted her face. "Yes'm. He called me this time."

"You seem to be doing better."

"Yes'm. That's the first time he ever did. Good night, Miss Favra."

"Good night, T'ling ... Oh, what do I do when we get there? I didn't see how you got in."

"Oh ... there's a bell on the right hand post as you go up on the porch. Ring it for five seconds then just barely touch it. The door will be unlocked and someone'll be there to take you in."

As she turned to enter the apartment she heard a hail. "A bright and happy good afternoon to you, Favra," called a cheery voice.

"Professor ... why, what has happened to you?"

"Oh ... just a few new feathers, my dear. Nothing like it to make an old rooster preen and strut."

"What happened, strike oil?"

He dusted an imaginary speck from his neat grey suit and his face grew sober. "May I beg a spot of alcohol? Ordinarily I do not indulge due to certain deplorable consequences during my youth but I feel especially festive today."

"Certainly. Come in."

She made him a highball and watched the appreciation light his eyes as he tasted it. "Tastes just as good as in the old days. The world is not going to hell as fast as many people my age would have it."

"You must have hit a streak of good luck, Professor?"

"You are a kind soul and I'm so happy to be able to retire my old black suit that I feel talkative. As you have no doubt guessed, I live on a very small income that is just about enough to keep me off the relief rolls. Sometime ago a well wisher who prefers to remain 'a friend' has been coming through with a few dollars every month, and welcome it is I can tell you. Today I get a letter signed from a friend *and* a friend. It seems that my popularity is growing, anonymously, of course. I received fifty whole dollars in good United States currency. Two twenties and a ten. Imagine getting all that cash in one hunk. Well, I went down on Rampart Street and badgered and dickered some loan shop owner out of an unredeemed perfectly fitting Kirchner suit that must have retailed new at close to a hundred and twenty-five dollars. Because it has a small almost undetectable rent in the knee I got it for twenty-five dollars."

Her eyes grew moist as the old man prattled on, almost beside himself with joy because he could look well again.

"So," he continued, "I stocked up on shirts and a few colorful ties. Black was never my color but it wears well and fades little."

"Professor," she said impulsively, "will you let me make you a loan? You can pay it back just as your income allows."

"Oh, no … no indeed." He flushed and looked embarrassed. "I couldn't allow you to do that, my dear. I live up to my income and as it fluctuates so do I. You are very kind but I couldn't let you do it."

"Well, I tried," she said smiling.

He stood up and considered her gravely for a moment. "There's nothing good enough for you in this world and if there was I couldn't get it for you. It is at times like this that impotent old men hand out good wishes. I do with all my heart wish I could give you something no other man in creation could. As it is, all I can do is stand here and make maudlin noises because I'm sentimental and easily touched."

"Don't you think I know that? Am I so dense that I can't see that I could have anything you could give me or wish for me?"

"I beg your pardon. Sometimes one becomes carried away with his own eloquence and forgets the obvious. You are not only a beautiful woman but a particularly intelligent one. And now I must be going. I'm going to stand myself to a dinner at Tujacques in honor of the occasion."

"Will you do something for me?"

"Anything, my dear, within my poor powers."

"Find Alice and take her, too."

His face went blank. "How odd it is that you should make that request. I was going to do just that but I wasn't going to tell anyone."

She took ten dollars from her purse. "Take this and you two have the dinner on me … please. I'm going to be hurt if you don't."

He sighed and took the bill reluctantly. "The way you put it I could hardly refuse. Very well. I …"

"And you won't tell her a word?"

His face wore a baffled look. "If you wish it. You know I find you enigmatic at times but never offensively so. There's always something noble lurking behind that face that could have launched more ships than that Greek trollop … what was her name … ? Helen. Well, thanks and good night."

She undressed, took a cold shower and dried vigorously with a rough towel. Then feeling relaxed and very comfortable she went into the bedroom and stretched out on the bed still naked and very conscious of a sense of physical well being. She must have fallen asleep because her doorbell shrilling made her get up with a start. She slipped on a robe of soft grey pile and went to open the door.

"I always say that a woman is always most beautiful when she is awakened from a sound sleep," said Aaron as he came into the living room. "What is the occasion for the daylight siesta?"

"I played tennis today," she said as she followed him into the living room. "I was tired and very much at peace with myself, something I haven't been for the last two weeks."

"In two weeks' time I'd say you've done nobly. I'm very much in tune with your moods. The instant I stepped in the door I felt it. What happened?"

"Oh … nothing drastic I suppose. I met a girl and for some reason we clicked instantly. I went home with her to lunch and saw what a rotten set-up she has to endure. The situation just burned me up and it apparently has done worse to her. She wants out and she wants me to teach her."

"Describe her," he requested, folding his hands and closing his eyes.

"Well, she isn't as tall as I …"

"A pity," he murmured. "Women should be tall. The pure pyknic type is too dull and foolish."

"And her skin is a good deal darker. She has the most gorgeous tan you ever saw."

"Capital … capital. Skin that is too white reminds me of a fish's belly, and it blemishes easily. Continue."

"She has a handsome face, rather on the strong side, and her lips are full and inclined to be petulant. As a whole her face is bafflingly lovely."

"Passion yet unborn. After its birth the lips become soft and gentle."

"Her hair is very fine and coppery, pretty dark but not titian."

"Titian and henna are too closely related to trust either. The picture grows."

"Well, she is strongly built and not as slim as I, but the beauty of her muscles, the way they glide under her skin when she plays tennis is marvelous. She has a truly patrician waist that moves in rhythm with her stride. It's almost sinfully attractive."

"Ah … there you have an almost infallible symptom of certain fleshly potentialities. Her stomach displays, I predict, a muscular activity that is delightful."

"I think so. She had on a T-shirt that covered her stomach but there was a suggestion of it."

"And now the things you have left till last. I can only assume in that particular field she surpasses you."

"Sometimes I think you are a witch doctor."

"I am merely a sensitive man. The barest emanation rings loud bells in my ears. Am I right?"

"I suppose so. They are larger, as they should be, considering her build, and as firm as apples."

"The analogy is apt if somewhat earthy. I should have said pomegranates. It is a more exalted fruit." He opened his eyes. "And when am I to see this disturber of an opium smoker's couch?"

"Soon. I made it possible, I think, for her to sully her feet in the Quarter, something she has been dying to do for a long time but she's watched like a hawk. By the way, we're to attend that performance I told you about."

"We are?"

"Yes, T'ling fixed it."

He took out a nail clipper and worked abstractedly on his fingernails for awhile. "Since Elton Chance stepped into your life you have become quieter and more serious. Did you know that?"

"No, I hadn't noticed. Maybe it's because I've been in low spirits and you've misinterpreted that as seriousness. I don't mind telling you that he started something that has made me lose sleep."

"Why don't you take another ferry ride?"

"Because I'd be running after him, which I'm not going to do."

"I think you're falling into a trap that is as old as man ... pride. If meeting him and his subsequent performance were as pleasant as you say then it would appear worth a little effort."

She sighed. "Let's not talk about him. I forgot him for a whole day today."

"The way to do the best job of forgetting is to find someone else worth remembering. Nothing has happened to you really except the initial flaw in female procedure known as emotionalizing sex. Elton Chance is attractive to you on the basis of two things. He is something of a boudoir buccaneer and he is unavailable. Either is enough to make you apply the emotional whip. With men it is different. They don't fall in love with every pretty girl with whom they sleep."

"I don't think there'll be any repetition of my feelings for Elton."

"Oh ... you talk like a love-sick adolescent, all this 'I'll never love again' chaff. You should know better. Find another man and become interested. Moping doesn't become you. One doesn't expect it of you."

He left a little later and when the door closed behind him she sat on the couch for a while, thinking. He had started a train of thought that was beginning to irritate her because she was now involved in a hot argument with herself. So what if I take a ride on the ferry? I probably won't meet him anyway, and if I do, I'll be cool and friendly without making a single move. If he makes one ... she stiffened, her whole body growing hot at the thought, a flood of saliva making her swallow jerkily. She shivered, pulled her robe closer, unconsciously, then realized that the weather was hot and she wasn't really cold. Tossing her tawny hair in irritation she got up and went into the bathroom, her mind made up. Aaron had suggested that if she couldn't conquer this feeling for Elton, then she'd better try to arrange another meeting. She bathed for the third time that day, touched herself about in spots with an expensive perfume, and put on a smartly tailored dress, the same that she had worn on the first meeting.

CHAPTER 6
ANOTHER FERRY RIDE

THE RIVER rolled silently on ignoring the thrashing of the ferry's paddle wheel, sending up strong steamy smells as before, titillating her nostrils and making her feel shivery and expectant.

On the Algiers side she stood against the rail and watched people stream on the vessel, but Elton was not among them. She sat on her bench again and smoked a cigarette while the cars pulled noisily aboard and were shunted into position by crewmen. Back to the New Orleans side again and when they docked she did not leave her seat. Soon after the ferry pulled away she heard footsteps coming up the companionway but thought little of them because it was likely that many people preferred to sit on the top deck although most of them liked the lounge and lower deck. The footsteps stopped and she could feel the slight motion of the bench as a heavy body sat down. "I had expected you before this."

She gasped and started, looking around. "Elton!"

She could see his grin in the lights of the dock that were still near enough to shed a faint illumination on the top deck. Her chin went up and her face came under control. "What do you mean you expected me before this?"

"Nothing, but isn't it the logical thing?"

"Not necessarily. I like to ride the ferry and you must have seen that I wasn't expecting anyone."

"Not even on the other side?"

She was silent, having been neatly trapped. It would do no good to deny it. "Very well, I came hoping I'd see you." She faced him. "It might have been a lot worse. I might have called you, I might have written. I might have tried in a more forward way to see you. I know who you are now so you needn't fall back on your laborer's speech."

He nodded. "I assumed you'd know by now. I'm not exactly unknown and a construction man is given a good bit of publicity."

She felt more comfortable now that all was in the open even if she had had to abandon her resolution to be cool and distant. "You're not angry because I tried to see you?"

"Oh no. I wasn't worried that you'd call, write or do anything that might cause me embarrassment. You see I have a lot of confidence in you because I think you're a level-headed, intelligent girl, only I wish you hadn't taken such a tumble."

She compressed her lips. "I certainly didn't expect to but you see I'm new at this sort of thing."

"I don't mind admitting that you made it pretty hard for me, too. I haven't had any better luck forgetting you than you have me. I know, however, that there can be nothing in this for you but further hurt, and that's why I didn't make it too easy for you to renew acquaintance."

"I don't understand. You're here, aren't you?"

The gentleness of his smile made her heart ache. "Yes, I'm here all right. Put it down to similar weakness on my part. I meant telling you about myself the way I did. That would have stopped some women."

She shook her head slowly. "It should have stopped me but it didn't. I don't seem to have a lot of control where you're concerned." She changed the subject abruptly. "Elton, tell me about your family."

"There isn't much to tell. The four girls are cute and saucy, the boys are my problem. One of them is a construction man dyed in the wool. The other is a dreamer, an artist, I guess you'd say, and so far hasn't done anything but write books that no one will buy, and keeps to himself a great deal. The first one is so immersed in business that he doesn't know how to live. He's a great help to me because I can duck a lot of details that he takes care of superbly, but the boy is a machine and all things take second place to work and money. I'm not like that and I wish he weren't. He'll take over the business some day and he'll have a lot of trouble."

"Sounds like he'd make quite a go of it."

"Lack of the human touch will make trouble for him. He wants me to fire all my men who are old and can't work as hard as they once did. Deadwood he calls them. He can't see that they are devoted to me and are a great help keeping new men in line. When I die he'll take over, clean house and get into trouble with labor."

"Can't you stop that … I mean, can't you make a provision in your will?"

"I thought of that but I'm going to do it differently. I'm going to set up a pension fund and then my old men won't have to put up with him. I could make him keep them on but he'd make it so tough they'd be forced to leave."

"I dislike him intensely," she said vehemently.

"What about the dreamer?"

"I don't know, but at least you haven't accused him of being cold and mechanical in his dealings with people."

"No. No one could accuse him of that. Sometimes I think he hates his brother."

"I don't wonder. I begin to sympathize with him."

"Few people do. The worker by his diligence and extroverted outlook makes friends a lot easier. You know the up and coming young executive type, the go-getter. They always gain the attention and sympathy."

"They're twins and that different?"

"Fraternal twins, not identical. I never saw two people so different."

"This sounds silly but I'd like to meet your family."

"You may, any time you desire."

"Oh … I may? But how would you explain me?"

"Don't worry about that. Tell you what! I'm having a few men and their wives in for dinner … let me see. This is Friday, isn't it? Well, it's a week off. Next Friday. Why don't you come?"

She shook her head. "Not to dinner. Will there be a party afterward?"

"Oh, yes. Dinner at my house always means a party."

"I'll come to the party … but I'll have to know why I'm supposed to be there."

He chuckled. "Just a lovely girl I bumped into and wanted my boys to meet. I've done that before."

"All right but I'm scared already."

"No need to be. We're just people in spite of what you may see in print." He put a hand over hers. The reaction stung her so badly that she snatched the hand away. "I'm sorry," she said. "You scared me."

"Was that why?"

"No," she said miserably. "I just can't stand to have you touch me the way things are."

He sighed and sat back against the bench. "I wish there were something I could do."

Favra heard her voice, as though coming from another source, against her will, throbbing with more of her heart than she ever allowed to show. "You could take me home and love me like you did the other night."

He was silent for awhile, and during the silence she built up such a roaring tide of excitement that she had to bite her hand to keep back a sound. Just having him near was bad enough, but to have him pondering over the question of the ecstasy that he would or would not give her was almost more than she could stand.

He turned to her. "My hesitancy was from the effort to try to figure it out. I can't. If you wish it I'll go to your apartment. You see, I'm a pretty soft individual myself. The thought of you as you were the other night is more than I can resist." With a sharp little cry she fell into his arms and began to weep, shaking so hard that he held her close for a long time.

"We're about to pull away from the Algiers dock," he said soothingly.

"Elton."

"Yes?"

"Let's go to the top deck … the roof."

The feel of the life floats was the same but his kiss seemed a thousand times sweeter, his arms more powerful and the ache to her ribs more intense and so weakening that she hung inert in his arms. Again she bit her lips to keep back a cry as the chill damp wind struck her bared thighs. Then the thunder of sensation, the roar of blood in her ears and the frenzied rhythm that gained strength and momentum, numbing her brain at length with a blinding flash of such joy that only her teeth sinking into the hard flesh of his shoulder prevented an outcry.

Elton shot the big convertible down dark streets.

The night was cool and old when at long last she was home and fell asleep. When she awoke, the sun was making a jail-window pattern on the carpet, shining through the venetian blinds. She sat up, yawned widely and hugged herself. She stretched on the bed again and relived the night. He had been right, she shouldn't have seen him again because he loomed larger than ever in her heart. She leaped from the bed resolutely and donned a pair of lavender flannel slacks and a white T-shirt. The morning being cool, she added a soft jacket of royal purple with a sash which she tied in a casual knot.

When she reached the French Market, the Professor, resplendent in new suit and linen, his new tie sparkling with color was already at the table and across the street she could see the shambling figure of Alice coming toward the coffee shop.

She returned the old man's wave and joined him. "My, but you are positively radiant this morning," she said with a smile.

"Fortune is smiling," he retorted, "why shouldn't I smile also … Ah, here is dear Alice." He leaped to his feet and assisted her into a chair.

"I'm peeved," said Favra pouting. "You didn't help me to my seat."

He flushed. "For that I must apologize. Youth, however, has an upsetting habit of helping itself to such an extent that with my slackening speed I would hardly be quick enough. Alice and I are more on a par."

"The child was only chaffing you," said Alice settling herself and throwing back her hood. "You needn't crawl and attempt to lick her feet."

Jesse came, took their orders and disappeared. Alice examined the girl with such a critical eye that she turned pink.

"Don't mind me, dear," said Alice with a chuckle. "I was taking silent inventory of your progress."

"I don't think I follow you."

"You asked me what I'd do if I were your age and had your money. You apparently have decided to heed my philosophy."

Favra examined her nails and was silent for awhile. "You didn't tell me that there were rocks in the road."

"Should I have? I thought most people knew that."

Favra laughed. "That, I think, will hold me for awhile."

"I find such discussions of questionable taste," said the Professor. "They make me uncomfortable."

"Then shut your ears," Alice told him. "Among friends there should be no conversational barriers."

"You speak better than any beggar woman I ever saw," said the Professor stroking his mustache and eyeing her critically.

"You speak well, too, and I'd make a small wager that the only classroom you ever were in, you were there as a student."

"That's right, Professor," put in Favra with a smile. "You sound like one but no one seems to know what school you taught in or what subjects."

The old man looked away. "Small denominational school up East . . . nothing, really."

"You're a poor liar," said Alice gently. "However, we'll respect your little romanticism if you wish."

"You should have seen her last night," said the Professor anxious to get to another less painful subject. "She was radiant."

"Oh, go along with you," said Alice patently pleased. "Since he has a new suit he's become even more extravagantly complimentary."

"I think that was nice, you two having dinner together."

"I'm still full," said Alice. "I hardly feel equal to breakfast."

As she spoke Favra noticed the look on the Professor's face, questioning, thinking hard as he watched the old woman. Jesse brought coffee and doughnuts and breakfast claimed their attention for awhile, but presently Alice pleaded the pressure of business, leaving them to their second cup of coffee.

"Professor, why were you looking at Alice like that awhile ago?"

He sighed, and lines showed in his face that she had not seen before. "It struck me last night. She had on a dress that while it was not chic or even pretty was better than that black horror she always wears, although it didn't fit any better. There's something strange about her. She has an arm that is as hard and large as mine, yet she gives the impression of being about to blow away. I don't understand it. Last night, to get along with what I was talking about, she reminded me of someone I once thought a great deal of. It was not only upsetting, per se, but it started me thinking about things I had all but forgotten, none of them pleasant. Do you want to hear a story?"

"Of course."

For half an hour he spoke, through another cup of coffee. In essence it was the same story she had heard from Alice. He seemed greatly relieved after the telling and in better spirits.

"So," he concluded, "I have explained some of the mystery of my past. I have never told it to another soul."

"That is a great compliment," she said softly. "Thank you for telling me."

His eyes misted a little. "Thank you for listening, my dear. You know, just by being around you make an old man very happy."

"And you think Alice is the girl you were in love with?"

"Oh, dear me, no. Yet somehow, last night she did seem to resemble her a lot. Maybe it is that I just imagined it. Alice was born in St. Louis and the girl I spoke of was born right here in New Orleans. Alice is a great deal older, too. I never knew what became of the girl." He raised his shoulders in a gesture of futility. "My family gave me the heave-ho about that time and I didn't have any money with which to search for her. She may be dead now."

"What would you do if you found her?"

He bit his lip. "How could I know? If she were successful and had money I would strive might and main to avoid her ... pride, I know, but I could never rid myself of it. If she were in my own position, financially, maybe we could still make a go of it, although I daresay two would starve quicker than one in spite of an adage to the contrary."

"Then you still love her?"

"There has never been a moment awake or asleep that I haven't loved her," he said passionately.

Favra took Aaron to the performance that night as she had promised, after which they went back to the apartment for drinks.

"The most amazing thing I ever saw," he said for the tenth time. "Such atmosphere, such beastly, primordial beauty, such fundamentality, such *performance.* It was the most savagely wonderful thing I ever saw … and that poor woman who lost her head and dashed into the fray. I felt especially sorry for her. I especially admire the Madam, whatever her name is. She is pure genius. Much goes on back of her eyes and did you notice how she watched me? Certainly she has seen people like me before."

"Possibly, probably, but you forget that you are something of an anomaly. You are not what you appear to be. T'ling said that the Madam seemed quite eager to have you come *after* she described you."

"Is that a fact?" He nodded slowly. "The Madam is quite a person herself. I think I'd like to know more of her. I should like to see more of her … in better light."

"Aaron!"

"And why not? As you know my primary demand of any woman is that she be beautiful. Now this Madam might be called more exotic than beautiful but they are difficult to separate at times … the phone, my dear."

She answered, listened to the rich contralto tones that sounded almost like a recording, and turned to Aaron. "It's for you."

He took the receiver with a languid hand and said, "Yes?"

"I see. Not at all. As a matter of fact, when you called I was discussing the matter with Miss McMullin, and at the same time wondering how I might meet you, er—socially. I can understand that, but why couldn't we meet … say, here? Miss McMullin is an excellent friend of mine and she gives parties to which you would lend no end of charm …" He raised his eyebrows at Favra who nodded. "Yes, so if you'll give me your number or one at which you may be reached I will be very glad to … One moment please. What is it, Favra?"

"Tomorrow night. I'm giving a party. It's Sunday and she won't be busy."

"Oh, er—Miss McMullin just told me that she was giving a party tomorrow night. We will be glad to have you if you can endure some of the weird characters who frequent these parties. Good, we'll expect you." He replaced the receiver. "She's coming."

"That was settled neatly," Favra said, draining her glass and lighting a cigarette.

"I like things neatly done," he said tapping one of his long cigarettes on a well manicured thumbnail. "This is more than intriguing. It is exciting."

"I should think so. Life is interesting for people who aren't manacled to codes and ..."

"Correction. People are people. They either fear deviations or they do not fear deviations. Mediocrity, where so-called normalcy abounds, breeds innumerable little fears and most mediocre people have invested so heavily in normalcy that they pop like a bladder at the thought of losing it. If they never lose it they are duller than dogs. Dogs are cute and perform tricks. The only thing such people do is look like other people, perform certain laborious routine jobs that enable people like you and me to live the way we choose."

"You must admit then that they are necessary."

He shrugged. "Maybe, maybe not. I don't know. They've been with us since time began and will always be with us. It is fortunate that they are good for something, else they would be dead weight."

"Some people might argue that you and I are useless."

"Then they would be ignorant. You and I are the goals toward which so many work, never appreciating such matters as personal limits, intrinsic differences and other things which often make their efforts futile."

She inhaled from her cigarette. "Would you say that you and I are happy?"

He cocked an eyebrow at her. "I'd say that we are content in a discontented sort of way. G.B.S. very pungently remarked once that he had no time for any such coma as that produced by happiness. Discontent has been the stimulant of all we have in a material way. Someone tirelessly searching for something, some nebulous Holy Grail, some state of being, some land of peace and happiness, never realizing that this very discontent would send them ever searching, on and on, no matter what they found."

"Then we are committed to a lifetime of searching, enjoying, and searching more?"

"In your case, I doubt it. You will some day snap up some healthy prancing stallion and start breeding. Little colts will appear in whatever numbers you desire and you will be so taken up with them that such safaris searching for diversion as you now take will not be necessary."

She put out her cigarette and faced him. "You know, for a person who is supposed to be this and that you do have the most logical outlook I ever saw. You predict motherhood for me and yet that will take me away from here probably and put me down in the middle of the very society with which I found it difficult to live."

"The difficulties will still be there," he said with a smile, "but you are not a Bohemian by birth. You bathe much too often, you have no pathological urge to make yourself ridiculous by bizarre deportment, and you're too level-headed, which is to say possessed of a balanced intellect. You are not stretched so far in one direction that you are distorted and made unfit for other directions."

At four the next afternoon she drove to the Drake residence to be ushered into the living room by Leslie who was almost simpering in his desire to please. "It is most delightful to see you again," he said as he pulled a chair toward her. "Please be seated. May I get you a glass of carrot juice, or would you prefer milk or pineapple juice?"

"Nothing, thank you. Will you tell Arden I've come for her?"

"Come for her ..." His brow darkened. "I'm afraid ..."

"I'm having a few people around to my apartment this evening and I want her to help me greet them. The guest of honor is Dr. Ashley J. Marcotte, the explorer and paleontologist."

"My ... my," he breathed. "Imagine meeting him. Oh, I'm certain that Arden will be delighted. Is Dr. Marcotte single?"

"I don't know but he is middle-aged. Arden wouldn't want to marry him, I'm sure."

"Arden will marry the man she is told to marry, Miss McMullin. We cannot afford to see the blood of the Drakes polluted with an inferior strain."

She leveled her eyes on him, hard and steady. "Leslie, this is not the middle ages, or hadn't you heard?"

He flushed. "I suppose we sound awfully brutal to you but you see, the Drakes are not ordinary people."

"In what way do they stand out?" she asked casually.

He floundered from the impact. "It is hard to make clear to another person ..."

"I should think it would be. In fact, offhand I could think up a few obstacles."

"You don't understand." He was very earnest now and leaned forward in his chair. "Our blood lines come down straight from British royalty ..."

"I thought Drake was a pirate."

Leslie turned almost purple. "He was knighted."

"Did that make him royalty?"

Leslie's breathing became labored. "I think I'll tell Arden you're here."

"Yes, do."

Arden came down almost immediately, her hair done upsweep, showing off the fine sculpture of her neck and displaying her lovely ears. Her make-up was restrained and flawlessly applied, making Favra tingle with appreciation.

"Miss McMullin wishes you to assist her tonight," said Leslie. "She is entertaining a very famous man and you should be honored."

"But I was …"

"Never mind what you were going to do," he interrupted brusquely. "You will accompany Miss McMullin. You will have an opportunity not afforded many girls of your age. Please attempt to conduct yourself honorably." Having given orders and seeing no opportunity to speak further with Favra he walked away.

They restrained their laughter till Favra pulled away from the curb then they broke into gales of mirth. "It seems a shame to pull the wool over his eyes like that," she gasped.

"Shame my aching tooth," retorted Arden. "Goody, goody, *goody!* I haven't been so tickled in years."

At Favra's apartment they had dinner early and went into the bedroom to dress. Arden, stepping naked about the room, entranced Favra.

"Gal, you have a figure that should get results so fast you might get run over."

CHAPTER 7
LESSONS IN LOVE

A RDEN SAT on the edge of the bed. "Do you think something might happen tonight? ... I hope not, because I want to get my feet on the ground and I don't want to appear too naive."

"Don't worry. Just don't let anyone get you alone. That's the secret. We're pretty blasé down here but we aren't performing in groups as yet."

Arden's face grew long. "Do you know that I've been kissed once in my life by a man?"

"My goodness ... I had no idea that you were so sheltered."

"That's the truth and I'm scared that I'll pull some silly stupid thing and make a fool of myself."

"You can't learn all at once ... it'll take time."

"Favra, what do boys do ... I mean, what should I expect? How do they make an approach ... Gosh, I don't know *anything*."

"Well, let's see what would be a good starting place." Favra frowned, thinking.

Arden sat straight, excited. "I know what, you play the boy and I'll be the girl. You just do what the boys do ... won't that be best? Better than just telling me, I mean."

The idea was intriguing, Favra had to admit. "Okay. I'll tell you. Put on my robe there and that'll be your clothes. Clothes make a difference and I doubt that you'll entertain in your bare skin ... not at the start anyway."

Arden blushed and slipped into the robe. "Where shall we sit, in the living room?"

"Yes. T'ling has gone, so it'll be safe. If she saw us she'd think we were crazy."

They sat on the couch and Favra said, "Now this will have to begin where he takes you into his arms. What happens before that is so varied that to attempt to project it would be useless. Once the clinch is applied though, there is a certain sameness, although it will also be quite varied." She put her arms around the girl. "Now comes the kiss and if you've been kissed only once it's likely to be a shock, but it'll be authentic." She covered the girl's soft lips with her own, gently at first then applied pressure. Her mouth was quiescent but unresponsive. She gave a twist that forced Arden's lips open and began to taste the tender underskin, nibbling it gently and burnishing it with her tongue. She could feel the girl's body go stiff and a little sound came from deep down. Working smoothly, she soon made her jaws open, their tongues met and Arden gasped audibly. They parted and Favra noticed that the other's breath was coming faster. "Usually there is a lot of this," she pointed out. "A really smooth operator is willing to take his time."

"I was imagining that you were a boy. I didn't have any idea that you'd really do that to me. It was wonderful."

"I salute your imagination. Now let's assume that you're starry-eyed from repeated sessions of what we just finished and maybe a quick but inoffensive something like this." She parted the robe and sank her mouth into the satiny surface of the girl's thigh, eliciting another gasp. She straightened up and noticed that Arden was starry-eyed. This, she thought, is getting good. The kid must have *quite* an imagination.

"Now," she continued, "you are all ready for the kill and under the spell of another kiss almost anything might happen."

She kissed her again, not surprised that this time the girl responded helpfully and her arms were strong, clasping her tight and holding her with a most ungirlish strength. Her tongue was sweetly hesitant at first then avidly helpful, her breathing now stimulated to a point that might have been a matter of pride for any wolf. Then Favra pulled her lips free and began to kiss the column of her throat, the latter caress fetching a little murmur of excitement and involuntary muscular movement, the girl's head going back in an ecstatic lurch against the couch.

Favra kissed her again, and this time brought a hand into play inching gently upward, hearing the little song of passion start in Arden's throat as the hand worked nearer with tantalizing slowness. Favra effected to become greatly stimulated, and in fact she was, to no little extent, being somewhat surprised by the fact. The kiss grew headier and more active as the hand moved slowly upward till at last Arden could stand it no longer and had to take away her lips to gasp for air. Then her body stiffened, bowed itself outward and her arms tightened painfully. Favra, whose intention it had been to stop, straightened up a little as a prelude but Arden pulled her back. "Please … please … Oh, Favra."

It was some minutes later and Arden sat in disheveled beauty, her robe half off and her hair that had come loose foaming in metallic glory about her creamy tan shoulders.

"Arden, something tells me that this is not the first time …"

"It isn't. Am I terrible?"

"My goodness no, why?"

"Because … Oh, I don't know but what is a girl like me to do? I don't have a normal life, no affection and … well, I needn't tell you anything about my nature. What else could I do?"

"When did you start it?"

"When I was twelve, I think. I just had to, I couldn't help myself."

"Forget it. It's a lot commoner among men than women and doctors say there's nothing wrong with it."

"But I've heard that it runs people crazy."

"You're not crazy, I'm not crazy. Many people with personality neuroses are found to do it because they find it impossible to meet society on equal ground and use it as a mean of escaping the frightening rigors of the real thing … frightening to them, I mean. Now, let's dress. It's getting late."

Arden was now a picture she would long remember. The dress was old but expensive and its fit, after they had done several things to it, could not have been improved. It was of a heavy white material that draped perfectly from the girl's shapely hips and fell in long folds. It had a wrap-around skirt with a very short square jacket that left several intriguing inches of tan skin available to the eye. Her hair was redone, accentuating her height, and the silver slippers that peeped from beneath the long skirt shone richly.

"Don't you think this is a little old or something?"

"Maybe," said Favra, "but I'd say the devil take style. You are a knockout. I don't think I ever really appreciated your true loveliness till now."

Tears came to the girl's eyes. "Thanks … thanks a lot. This night has meant a lot. You have no idea what my kind of living has done to me. This is like walking out of jail, although I know I must return."

"Then you can get out all over again. That'll be fun."

The doorbell rang and Favra, dressed in a clinging hostess gown of pale dusty blue went to answer it. For a moment she thought the ringer had mistaken an address then recognition gradually filtered through. "Oh …. I'm sorry; I didn't recognize you for a moment. Do come in."

"Thank you," the woman said, walking into the living room with easy grace. Her dress was dull red moire taffeta with a gold link belt that looked rich and heavy. A black velvet cape trailed from her shoulders. She sat on the couch and looked up. "I'm early, I know, but I promise not to get in the way. You were most kind to let me come."

"Why, I'm delighted to have you," said Favra earnestly. "I really don't know your name."

"No one does," said the woman showing ivory white teeth in a slow attractive smile. "When it is necessary to use a name I'm called Esta Parvenue."

"That's good enough for me, Esta. Everyone has a name but we never know whether it is the one their parents gave them. No one ever asks around here at any rate."

"That is kind of you. You are probably wondering why I made an effort to see the little man."

She smiled. "Aaron is an immensely entertaining person. That you became interested is not strange, and as far as I know, he is without a counterpart."

"That is the intriguing thing about him. I've seen men like him before, physically, but they always avoided women... for reasons we can understand."

"Shall I fix you a drink?"

"Not at the moment. May I examine your apartment? It is lovely."

"The way to my heart is through my apartment. After the luxury of your own if you can notice mine I'm flattered."

The woman stood up and approached a picture on the wall. "This is a Delaire, is it not?"

"Only a copy of one Aaron has. Are you acquainted with his work?"

Esta smiled slowly. "In an amateurish sort of way. He paints things that make sense so I suppose the professionals consider him a crass commercialist."

"You'll pardon me now. I have a few things to do yet and I have a guest in the bedroom."

"Go by all means. I apologize again for coming so early but ..."

"I take that as a high compliment," said Aaron coming through the door. "Run along, Favra, and I'll entertain our guest. Now, my dear, what may I call you?"

"Esta ... and I take it that you're Mr. Festival."

"Aaron ... let us not stand on formality. Shall I construct two drinks instead of one? You'll love Favra's bourbon. It is unsurpassed."

"It is a bit early but I might as well. Miss McMullin tells me that you have an original Delaire."

"Yes. One of my more prized possessions. The one you see on the wall there is a copy of mine and done with such impeccable care that if they were mixed I wouldn't be able to separate them. It is a pity that the man, who by the way you will meet tonight, has to slave impecuniously, copying, when he has such talent. I will say for him though that he copies and does not attempt to do revolting daubs without form or shape and scream to heaven that they are true art and everything else is either commercial trash or mechanical draughtsmanship." He handed her the drink, sat beside her on the couch and stroked the ivory leather with a delicate forefinger. "Would it be an offense at this early hour to give voice to a mild curiosity?"

She smiled a slow tantalizing smile. "I am as impervious to the petty niceties of conduct as you are to the penetration of ugliness into the fields of beauty."

His glance was quick and sharp. "Something tells me that you are no ordinary person, if I may be bold and conservative at the same time."

"Had I been, would you have accepted my rather brassy advances?"

"Doubtless not. I might point out for your edification that women who are not beautiful bore me to distraction. I will have no traffic with them."

She gave him a little bow. "I'm properly complimented."

"That will come later," he assured her. "Right now I am endeavoring to get us on a solid conversational basis. Later I have some gems ... for your ears alone."

"Then we will be alone?"

"Naturally, unless you find me such a bore that you feel unequal to the task of enduring me."

His eyes met hers steadily then they calmly devoured every line of her lithe, marvelous figure. They came back to her face and studied the fine bony structure, the depth of her almost black eyes, the jet glory of her hair that had been put up in braids, wound tiara-like about her well shaped head.

"Do I please you?" she asked with another slow smile.

"Immensely, and you are a delight in other ways as well. Another might have become offended at my scrutiny."

"I'm flattered. May I say in return that although you do not have the shoulders nor the narrow hips of the godlike figure, and though your face is smooth and the skin pretty, I have conceived a liking for you that pressed me to making the request to see you?"

He laughed. "I dare say that there are other things of which you have heard that also made you wonder just what sort of oddity I might be."

"I will not deny it. You are outside my experience and I am curious."

"I think we shall get along famously. Neither of us has any respect for the futility of gesture. We are realists. I should say that we will be friends."

"That will be an experience. I hadn't realized, till you mentioned friends, that I have none."

"Then I suggest certain points of starvation. You must be hungry."

Her eyes seemed to burn hotly and her voice was husky. "You cannot have any conception how hungry or how determined I am to go hungry no longer."

His eyes were bright. "Rest easily, my dear, rest easily. We shall see what we shall see."

Favra and Arden came out, there were introductions, after which Esta asked permission to repair her face and went through the bedroom into the bath.

"What an attractive person," breathed Arden.

"Ummm," murmured Aaron, his eyes on her bare midsection. "Tell me, what exercise do you take besides tennis?"

She flushed at his frank scrutiny. "I've taken dancing..."

"Acrobatic?"

"Yes."

"That accounts for the wonderful musculature of your stomach. Will you favor me, my dear, by walking slowly to the bedroom door, turning and coming back here?"

Arden flashed a glance at Favra who nodded and smiled. "Bear with him and do as he says. He is admiring you. He wishes to watch the music of your rear."

"The... my *what?*"

He smiled disarmingly. "You see, I find music in all beauty, silent sometimes but music nonetheless. I wasn't watching you closely when you came in. I'd like to see you repeat the entrance. Walk naturally, do not change your natural stride by one iota."

Astounded as she was, she felt a quick flash of liking for this effeminate little man. He was obviously Favra's friend and... she took a quick irritated breath. She was acting like a wide-eyed adolescent... Turning she walked slowly back, her face flaming as she suddenly realized that with a little accentuation she might resemble a street walker approaching a prospect. Aaron's smile was gentle.

"Superb," he breathed. "Favra, this delightful morsel presents a worthy challenge to your hitherto unapproachable station. Arden, did you know that if you walked through the Senior Business Men's Club as you just did, at least ten of them would die of apoplexy?"

Arden felt a delicious bubbly sensation rise to her throat but she restrained it to a modest laugh. "You make me feel like a nude exhibit in a Persian slave market, Mr. Festival."

"You may call me Aaron and may I say that if you ever appeared in such a slave market it would cause a desert war that would take all the genius of Ralph Bunche to quell."

Others started dropping in and in an hour the party had begun to gather momentum. There was Denver Dawson, the cadaverous copy artist with his long bitter face, and eternal cigarette hanging limp between his thin lips. Marta Mavern, a brilliant pianist currently headlined at a plush Quarter club. She was a small blonde who ceased talking only when she played the piano. Aaron disliked her because her incessant yammering irritated him.

With her was a small man with a waxed moustache and pomaded hair that smelled loudly, offending Aaron's sensitive nose.

There was Lucy St. Dennis, a large-boned woman with lusterless black hair and dirty nails stemming from her hobby of raising flowers.

"She," said Aaron aside to Favra, "has a nature that is beautiful if her body is gross. She coaxes flowers from the earth and transforms them into a joy to the eye. I love her."

"What," asked Favra taking advantage of the respite, "do you think of my protegé?"

"Your protegé is without a doubt the most scintillant creature you ever had in this house excepting yourself."

"Still loyal?"

"Certainly and what do you think of my girl?"

"She is certainly exotic and she has managed to coax Denver from his bitter reflections."

"A matter not to be sneered at. I can't get over the poetry of Arden's walk. It is the sheerest witchery, as Merry Ballard apparently has found out."

"Yes, I noticed that Merry hasn't left her side for a moment. Is he dangerous?"

"He is a man, a very masculine man, and that I think should answer your question. Lofton Kramm seems to wish he were in Merry's shoes at the moment."

The sculptor was leaning on the grand piano, heedless of the gushing Chopin being rendered by Marta, his earrings glinting and his gaze rapt, fixed unwaveringly on Arden and Ballard. Ballard was a big good-natured fellow, buoyant and boyish, who did exquisite pastels and received exorbitant prices for them. He was not the popular conception of an artist except for the mop of heavy, taffy blond hair that, in spite of his best efforts, kinked and curled in wild profusion. His eyes were bright blue, his smile eager and personable, his shoulders tremendous and his torso kept in trim by rigorous exercise.

"I'd say that Merry has the inside track, wouldn't you?"

"What would you expect? I can smell Kramm from here and there isn't another man about who could even make Merry get up a sweat, speaking in terms of rivalry … By the way, I'm taking Esta to my house for a nightcap after we leave here."

"Where a great time will be had by all."

"That is in the arms of the future. Offhand, I'd say yes."

Favra walked back in the kitchen to arrange the food that T'ling had prepared and placed in the icebox. She could feel Aaron's eyes upon her as she walked, and if she accentuated the smooth sinuous roll of her hips the least bit it was done consciously for his express benefit. Even so Denver Dawson also saw and followed her into the kitchen. "How," she asked, "did you escape from your ivory siren?"

"By the simple expedient of leaving her to the mercies of Aaron whose intention it appeared was to follow you. Instead he came over to us and invited himself to our discussion of painting."

"Did you resent his intrusion?"

"Oh, no. Quite to the contrary. I was rapidly approaching the admission that I am not an artist at all but a mechanic with a certain innate familiarity with tubes and brushes but without the slightest imagination or originality."

"I think you are unnecessarily brutal to yourself."

"A masochist," he murmured with even more brutality.

"Did you notice my co-hostess?"

"Who could help it?"

"Very well. She is not a painting but a live warm-blooded animal with an exquisite, unspoiled natural beauty. Of course, she is, in a physical sense, the product of someone else, but if you could copy Delaire so beautifully why couldn't you copy Arden Drake ... say, in the nude?"

She could hear the knuckles of his long fingers crack as he contracted them. "I prefer my own brand of brutality, my dear, if you don't mind. We are friends, so to speak. I know what to expect from it. What you just did is infinitely more cruel. To be frank, I never had the nerve to ask anyone to pose for me ... in the flesh."

"I mentioned it merely to suggest something. You eat yourself to bits inwardly and say you have no originality, yet you are a copyist without equal. Very well, why not take a body like hers and copy it. If you did a good job, think what it might mean."

Denver sat down and cracked his fingers. "I wish you wouldn't give me hope like that. Despair when it is fairly complete and final has its points of comfort. The thought of leaving it then having to come back is unendurable. Do you think she would pose for me?"

"I have no idea. Why don't you ask her?"

"No nerve." He lit a cigarette from the butt of the previous one and leaned back. "You see, I hate myself afresh because of no nerve."

Favra arranged cheese, olives, crackers and tiny rounds of salami on a big platter then turned to Denver. "Where are you headed?"

"Just where you think. One of these days I'll find enough nerve to take a fistful of sleeping pills."

"That should take a great deal more nerve than asking a naive girl to pose for a painting."

"You're being logical. No one should attempt logic with an artist."

"I thought you said you were a mechanic."

"Favra, you are determined to crucify me, aren't you?"

"No. I like you and I think you have the elements of great-ness...how old are you?"

He chuckled bitterly. "Thirty and don't let it throw you into a faint. I know I look sixty."

"You look a lot older than thirty, I'll admit that."

"Why," he asked suddenly, "don't you pose for me? I do not for a moment admit that Arden is your superior."

"I'm ordinary," she said slowly, choosing her words carefully. "I'm just good, Arden is simply unbelievable. You are an artist, didn't you catch the emanations, the luminosity, the deep-seated dynamism...?"

He ground out a laugh. "You sound like a surrealist trying to explain his work."

"No, I mean it...Denver, I'll ask her for you. Would it take long? I'm asking that because she is confined and wouldn't have a lot of time."

He shook his head. "For some, but not me. I could sketch her in half an hour. Three more sittings of that and I'd have enough to put out the product. I have a camera mind and don't have to stare at the model all the time. I paint like an amateur writes. I look and paint furiously until the image fades. Then I look back. I'm really too fast to be any good."

"I don't accept that. I'll ask her."

The sight of food temporarily suspended conversation and drinking as they crowded around the table helping themselves and making complimentary remarks about the snack. "Who is the cook?" asked Marva with her mouth full of deviled egg.

"A gold and ivory figurine named T'ling," supplied Aaron, nibbling daintily at a strip of pungent Romano. "An escapee from the mother-of-pearl halls of some fabulous harem."

Marva giggled and continued to stuff herself, earning a disgusted glare from Aaron who turned and handed an hors d'oeuvre to Esta. "You appear ill," she said smiling.

"I am," he replied bitterly. "Marva has the fingers and ankles of an angel, her hair is a dream of spun gold but her brain would feel lonely within the confines of one small thimble. A waste of excellent material."

"Are you partial to blondes with spun gold hair, trim ankles and fine fingers?"

His head shake was faint. "No.... I'm partial to beauty. I despise to see it wasted."

"Aaron..."

"Yes?"

"Let's find a little corner and eat in relative peace. We haven't had an opportunity to talk."

"By all means. Would you rather leave now?"

"No, I'm having fun and the night is young yet. I haven't been to a party in so long."

There was a little back porch off the kitchen and Aaron found chairs for them there. It was dark and very cozy with a cool breeze blowing.

"What do you think of our friends?"

"I can see intelligence, talent, beauty, stupidity, tension and unhappiness, yet they all seem to be searching madly for happiness."

Favra coming into the dark kitchen for a drink of water heard them and paused to listen. Esta had risen and a shaft of light from some distant street lamp threw a crooked shape across the upper part of her body. Aaron's finger came out of the dark and touched the line of her jaw, slowly tracing it then touching her lips. Favra heard the indrawn breath and saw Esta's eyes close as she leaned against the door facing.

"Starved..." Aaron spoke the one word and bent his head to taste the deep cleft between her breasts. Esta's slim hand came back of his neck and urged him closer making Favra duck silently back in the living room where she hoped her face did not betray her.

Merry Ballard had sought Marva, leaving Arden somewhat at a loss, uncomfortable and ready to take a drink much too large for her youthful capacity. "Who," asked Favra looking at her accusingly, "fixed that drink for you?"

Arden glanced at it. "Why...Merry fixed it, then made an excuse and went to talk to Marva."

"Here, give it to me."

"Why, what's the matter with it?" She handed the drink to Favra who tasted it.

"Whew...were you ever about to be slugged? I don't like Merry for that. Now listen to me, Arden. Stay away from him. Go talk to...no, you stay here and someone'll come to you. Just lay off Merry."

"But he's..."

"I know exactly what he is. He'll be proposing a walk before you know it and with a drink this size inside you you'd be led to the slaughter like a lamb."

"I'm sorry...I didn't mean to be..."

"Dry up, infant. You're learning. Just listen to Aunt Favra till you have your sea legs. Denver Dawson wants you to pose for him."

"He does?...Oh, how nice..."

"In the nude."

Arden's expressive face became a racetrack of various emotions. "...In the nude?" Her voice was almost a whisper. "Would it be...I mean...Do you think...."

"Do you want to know what I think?"

"Yes, please...."

"Do it. Denver is shy, defeated, and wouldn't touch you with a ten-foot paint brush. Actually, if he does a job on you, you might become as famous as Nana."

Arden's face paled for a moment then her jaw tightened...hard. "Oh, I'd die with joy if I could make my parents go to an exhibit and see me there...without a stitch on...Do you think..."

"I don't *know,* naturally, but I certainly do think."

Arden's eyes sought Dawson where he sat near the piano listening, plainly bored, to Lofton Kramm explaining something, using both hands to drive home his points. Favra caught his eye and inclined her head in their direction. Muttering something and leaving Kramm in the midst of a violent gesture he got up and approached them.

"Arden has agreed to pose for you, Denver."

Dawson swallowed hard and nodded. "I…am…overwhelmed."

He was. It was obvious and Arden felt a quick stab of pity for him because he was acutely uncomfortable. "I'm the one who is overwhelmed, Mr. Dawson. When shall I come?…I suppose Favra told you…"

Dawson's deep eyes began to smoulder. "Miss Drake, any time you come to my place I'll be glad to drop whatever I'm doing and work on you. It will take very little time, really. As I told Favra I'm too fast to ever be really good."

Arden's smile was so brilliant as to be virtually audible. "And she has said that you will make another Nana of me."

"Not like Zola either," put in Favra slyly.

Dawson blushed furiously. "Some day I'm going to throttle you."

"You will not. You will bow down at my feet and kiss the hem of my dress."

"I'll do that now," he countered boldly, recovering somewhat. "What you have just done places me under a heavy obligation."

"You may escape by making me a copy of your painting of Arden. That's all I ask."

"You shall have it. When can you come, Miss Drake?"

"Please call me Arden because I'm going to call you Denver. I'll come whenever I can get away. I'm fairly free, days. Nights I'm watched like a hawk."

"Any day, any time at all …"

"What momentous decision has just been reached?" asked Aaron as he and Esta came into the room.

"Secret," replied Favra, taking a swift, all-inclusive glance at Esta who was as calm and mysterious as before but her cheeks were rosy, her respiration not yet steady, and her eyes smoky pots of fire.

"I dislike secrets; I am very angry and Esta and I will vacate your domicile at once."

"What a pity. We were thinking of asking you to give a rendition of the Gettysburg Address."

"Pooh and fie … seriously, it has been a nice party and we appreciate your hospitality. May we come again?"

"Whenever you choose, as you well know. Quit showing off before Esta."

"You crush me …"

Esta stepped forward and shook hands with Favra. "Please accept my thanks for a wonderful evening … and come to see me …"

"I shall. I have someone else I'd like to bring."

"Do so, by all means … you will be my guests this time."

Marva's friend had become angry at her attentions to Merry and left in a huff and now others came to speak to the hostess and say good night.

Merry and Marva stayed as did Denver who had not left Arden's side since the painting had come into discussion. He was in animated conversation with her. Lofton Kramm somewhat left out at first came over to Favra, a smile on his lips.

"Sorry you have to go, Lofton," she said in an attempt to forestall anything he might have on his mind. The smile disappeared to reappear again with less conviction. "Er … well, yes. Getting a little late, you know … nice party."

She sighed as she closed the door behind him. That had been neatly done; now if Merry and Marva … They rose and came toward her. "We gotta slope, kid," said Merry. "Monday morning and all God's chillun gotta work."

"We did have a nice time," chattered Marva. "And I just love your piano and your friends…" She looked up at Merry and the look made Favra contract inwardly. Never had she seen such naked lechery shine from anyone's eyes. Merry put an arm about her, making the girl shudder and sway against him.

"Think you can wait?" asked Favra, still somewhat put out that Merry would attempt to slug Arden, then pass her up for a sure thing.

He flushed while Marva put on a mechanical smile and held it not knowing exactly what the whole thing was about. As they passed out of the door Favra saw Marva make an advance that sent a shaft of freezing sensation through her and she slammed the door harder than she intended. She shook her head and walked back to Denver and Arden. "May we drop you some place when we go? I've got to take Arden home."

He glanced at her reproachfully, sighed and stood up. "No, thanks. I have to walk… I should walk. I don't get enough exercise. Thanks for the night, Favra. I really mean that."

"I know you do, Denver. Good night."

Arden fell back on the couch and kicked off her shoes. "Favra, this has been such a wonderful night. Do you think I'll have the nerve to take off my clothes in front of him?"

"Of course you will… but I'll be there if you wish."

"Please… the first time, anyhow. I'll need a lot of moral support. The strangest thing… he fascinates me and I'm sorry for him all at once. I thought he was ugly when I first saw him and now I don't think so at all. Is that strange?"

"Not necessarily. You admire him because of his talent and you feel sorry for him because of his fears and lack of self confidence."

Arden leaned forward. "I tried to boost his ego and you should have seen him beam. He appreciated it so much."

Now this, thought Favra, has developmental possibilities. Arden doesn't recognize symptoms but I do. I'd say she's just what Denver needs.

Later when Arden stood before the long mirror with her clothes off she said, "You know everyone here tonight, almost everyone that is, made me conscious that I have a body and that it can excite people."

"That is a step in some direction or other."

They pulled up beneath a giant oak and Favra braked the car to a stop.

"Leslie is up ... that's funny. He's in bed this time of night usually."

Favra grinned. "When we go in you go on up and leave me with him. Later you sneak back down ... I may need you."

Arden's hands clenched in her lap. "That would be the final clincher. If I could *ever* catch Leslie making a pass ..."

"Try it. I'll bet on the results although I did want to beat him at tennis. I can forego that pleasure in your favor."

Leslie let them in, his thin face alive with a smile. "Do come in, Miss McMullin." He ignored Arden who said good night and went up the stairs without looking back.

"Will you sit down for a few minutes? I'd like to talk to you ..." Leslie was nervous and ill at ease but he managed a certain gallantry taking her to the couch. He sat beside her and fiddled with the fastenings of the robe he wore.

"Er ... was the party a success?"

"Oh, yes. Dr. Marcotte was *so* interesting."

"I can imagine ... I can imagine. Did Arden conduct herself well?"

"Impeccably." He was visibly impressed. "You have a lovely sister, Leslie."

"Not half as lovely as you." He leaned forward, his voice strained and she smelled toothpaste on his breath, for which she was thankful.

"That's because she's your sister," she said laughing. "I can't touch her in looks."

"You are enough to drive a man mad," he said huskily, leaning closer. She laughed throatily and touched his face with her hand. "You're nice to say so, Leslie."

"Oh, but it's true." He got up and turned out a light leaving only one dim table lamp burning. "Hurts my eyes," he explained lamely.

He sat closer this time, placing his arm on the back of the couch and letting it slip down on her shoulders, accidentally. She did not make a move because she could tell that he was in a fever of excitement and any opposition might snap him out of it.

"Why were you never married?" she asked.

"Never wanted to ... till now. Miss McMullin, you are an intelligent sophisticated woman and I ..."

He stopped, all atremble from the enormity of what he was about to say. She turned her face toward him, very close. "Yes?"

"I mean to say ..." He ran a finger around the inside of his collar as though it were choking him. "What I mean is ..." He stopped again and she placed a soft palm against his cheek. "What, Leslie?"

Her voice was cooing, soft, and sank gently into his blood bringing it to a fast boil.

"You drive a man mad ... mad."

"Why, Leslie, what a thing to say." His arm tightened and drew her closer.

"I mean it. I haven't been normal since you came to lunch that day. I've got to have you, Favra ... you'll pardon me if I call you Favra ... won't you?" A frenzied shiver shook him and his breath rasped hungrily in his throat.

"You don't even know me," she chided. "You've never even kissed me."

Roughly he drew her closer and found her lips. She threw every bit of energy and finesse at her command into the kiss, and had his mouth been free, he would have squealed. As it was he sounded like a puppy being smothered. She stroked the back of his head, his ears and drew her hands across his neck making him writhe as though in exquisite pain.

"Oh, God … Oh, God …" He buried his face in her hair and held her with such strength as to almost stop her breathing. "You gorgeous, marvelous creature … Oh, God …" He found her lips again and this time essayed a very bold maneuver with his hand that in spite of her rather detached state of mind sent a thrill through her. The thought struck her that it might even be fun to … No, there was Arden for whose benefit this was being arranged and true to her schedule she appeared. His hand had assumed a dangerous position and she made pointedly futile efforts to block it but he was in a state of madness now, his caresses not to be balked, and when the overhead lights went on they were in a very compromising position.

"I heard noises," said Arden in a brittle voice as she walked toward them. Favra straightened up and pulled her dress down, affecting to sob bitterly. "He did it, Arden … he did it. I tried to stop him … I tried …"

"Say no more, my dear." She faced her brother who was in a sort of comatose haze that was rapidly turning into blind panic.

"To say that I'm horrified, to say that I'm stunned, Leslie, would be a half truth at best. My guest, my own house, my own brother."

Leslie, pale, his face dewed with sweat made a despairing gesture with a hand and a hoarse croak came from his throat.

"The way you've talked," she continued inexorably. "The preachments and the moral shouting you've hurled at me … and the time you saw me kiss Edward Pennington. You told Father and I had to stay in my room for a week. Now this! Tell me, dear brother, what have you to say for yourself?"

Leslie let a trembling hand flutter over his face. A peep like that of a frantic chicken came from his throat and, tottering to his feet, he almost ran from the room.

Favra and Arden collapsed on the couch and laughed silently, their shoulders shaking and their eyes streaming. Arden raised her head and wiped her eyes.

"I'll love you the longest day I live. You have at last emancipated me. I have a whip in my hand now and I'll use it whenever I choose."

For three days Favra stayed home, writing letters, taking short strolls through tropical moonlit nights but seeing no one save the Professor and Alice in the mornings. One night when she was about to go for a walk from sheer restlessness her bell sounded and she admitted Aaron.

"Ah ... divinity and no less. What material is that negligée?"

She smoothed the silken stuff against her hips. "I don't know, some synthetic I think. Like it?"

"With you in it ... ? What a thing to ask."

"How is your romance?"

He chuckled. "As little as you might suspect, it appears that at long last romance has come into my life. She's wonderful. She is a siren of jet, rose and marble, and if she was surprised to find me then I am no less surprised to find a woman like her. I find myself getting lonely when she isn't around."

"I think that's wonderful. I'm so glad for you."

A look of intense distaste came over his face. "You make me feel unworthy and I do not like to feel that way. Do you realize that you are always concerned with other people's troubles? What are you doing for Favra?"

She smiled. "I'm attending a party at the home of Elton Chance, Friday night."

"Oh, Lord ... you're chaffing me."

"I'm not, it's a fact."

His laugh was incredulous. "What is it you *can't* do?"

"I can't have Elton. Aaron, I'm afraid."

"Of whom, pray tell, and I'll murder the bastard with a hatpin."

"Can you see me walking into Elton's big house, meeting his friends, his wife, his sons…?"

"Oddly enough I can. I can see you sweeping into the place, so lovely that the most oaken heart in the place will ache, charming everyone and making every other one fall in love with you. Those who don't will want to put you up in an apartment and pay your bills."

CHAPTER 8
A CHANCE MEETING

I T WAS Friday night, the entrance had been gracefully effected, the wife and friends greeted without any loss of poise. Mrs. Chance was a well-preserved woman, very capable, very intelligent and very wise, so wise that Favra wondered if she were giving away something. Elton was magnificently dressed and very debonair, while a number of his friends and their wives looked at her with mixed emotions.

"Elt and Borden haven't come in yet," said Chance. "Elt is always the life of the party when he can get his head out of figures, but Borden is another matter. Maybe he'll come to the party and maybe he'll go to his room and remain there."

"Borden," put in Elissa Chance, "is a very sensitive boy, Miss McMullin. I hope you will not be offended if he seems a trifle abrupt and hard to know."

Elton boomed out a laugh. "She didn't throw me off the ferry when I asked her for a light that afternoon so she won't mind him."

Favra smiled. "Your husband has such ingratiating ways. He made it sound as though I'd be doing him a vast favor if I gave him a match. Does he always go around picking up girls?"

Elissa chuckled delightedly. "He's been doing it for years. He just simply loves pretty girls and can't help it. He's fairly honest about it. Now he says he collects them to show off to Elt and Borden. I say he does it for the same reason he always did."

"Come now," begged Elton. "Let's go on in where they are getting a Canasta game going. Play, Favra?"

She shook her head. "I like to talk. I never play card games."

"You'll find someone to talk to."

She did and was amused when a fat bald-headed man whom she took to be a department store executive offered her the apartment that Aaron had prophesied. She was about to have a little fun with him when a blond giant of a man burst into the room and boomed a hello to everyone. She hoped later that she hadn't seemed too stupefied when they were introduced because Elt was his father's image, much younger and handsomer but without the older man's placidity. Her heart was hammering heavily and when the face of Borden swam into view it passed without much impression. She remembered that where Elt's face was broad and red bronze, the other's was rather thin with a mop of curly black hair. Both were large, she remembered, about the same size, but finding another Elton available drove everything else out of her mind. The rest of the night was a fog through which faces swam, faces that meant nothing, faces whose identity she could not remember … none but Elt's. He was very attentive and seemed to sweep her into the forefront of his brilliant conversation, usually about construction work, quick figures on the tip of his tongue from whence he fired them with machine gun rapidity. It was intoxicating to sit and listen to him, watching his great hand crushing the arm of a chair while he sat tensely on the edge delivering monologues, yet admitting others into the conversation in order to deliver even more devastating broadsides of logic spiced with wit and authority. In the kitchen Borden sat sipping a glass of beer and eating a thick sandwich of barbecued beef and sharp mouldy cheese the aroma of which sent delightful little splinters of smell through the room.

Elton walked in, wrinkling his nose. "When you get through eating, if there's any left, bury it."

Borden raised cynical eyes to his father. "You're still a clod, Pop. This cheese is delicious."

Elton grunted and sat down. "Your brother is his charming self tonight."

"Isn't he always?"

"I guess so. Any luck with the books?"

Borden laughed harshly. "Need you ask? Writing is a tiresome and slow-moving thing. I have hopes."

Elton poured a stiff shot of whiskey and tossed it down. "I wonder if I did right asking that girl to come here."

Borden stopped chewing and looked at the older man keenly. "Why do you say that?"

"Because Elt is throwing up the snow job of his career right now and she's eating every word."

"If she is, then she's an idiot. She doesn't deserve any better."

"That is where you're wrong."

The bottomless gray eyes came up again and looked at the father for a moment. "Tell me, Pop, what about these girls you bring around every now and then. I've noticed that they seem to think you're a sort of god."

Elton lit a cigarette and didn't answer immediately. "What you're saying is that I'm a killer with the women. I'd have to be to be ... god to them."

"It has been done. I knew a fellow at school who slept with every girl who'd stay still long enough and they thought he was a prince. He never seemed to break hearts. That is nothing less than sterling genius."

"And you think I have it?"

"I didn't say. I was speculating."

Elton's eyes were as steady as rocks. "I'd tell you because you don't have a dragline for a mind. I will tell you if you insist."

Borden drank the last of his beer. "Pop, you're the best father a guy ever had. You have your weaknesses but you never become self-conscious about them and get hypocritical and sanctimonious. You don't hate Elt because he's such a fool and you don't hate me because I'm a dreamer, a waster of time … and *not* a construction man. That last must have taken a lot of self-searching. Fathers always want their sons to follow the line."

"I may have felt that way once but now I am beginning to believe that you know more about life, people and living than the rest of us. We should envy you, not feel sorry for you."

"Thanks, and of course, you're right. Are you afraid for the kid?"

"Frankly, I am."

"Then I'll take her home."

"It isn't that simple. I'll be frank with you, Borden. That girl came to this house in love with *me.* It was simple in this case to transfer it to Elt. He looks like me and has a lot more drive and fire."

The son lit a cigarette and broke the match stem into small pieces hurling them forcefully into a trash can. "No one could ever accuse you of passing up life. I can see where some of me came from. Not all but some. What will you do?"

"I don't know. Maybe she'll weather the storm."

"Ships do and still get grounded with all hands washed overboard and the masts off at the deckline."

"I hope it won't happen this time. She's a wonderful girl. She deserves better."

"Me, perhaps?"

"Perhaps. I had thought about it and tried to prepare her for Elt's impact but I might have saved my breath."

"I work in devious ways, Pop, and she's a knockout. I'll see what it means to meet Elt head-on."

"Think you could love her?"

"I don't know."

"Then leave her to hell alone." Veins stood out on Chance's forehead from the force of his ejaculation.

Borden raised his eyebrows ironically. "You going to tell Elt that, too?"

"Son, don't *you* misunderstand me. I couldn't stand that. You know what I mean."

Borden felt a quick stab of feeling and he gripped his father by the arm. "Pop, how much money are you going to leave me when you die?"

"An equal portion ... why?"

"Let me have it now or part of it so I can get out of here. I'll come back sometimes and you and mother can come see me from time to time. I'll watch out for the girls like always and I'll see them, but I can't stay here any longer. I've had about all I can take of my loving brother. If I stay I might poison him."

Elton sighed heavily. "I had hoped it wouldn't come to this but maybe it is just as well. Where'll you go?"

"To the French Quarter. I won't leave town. Beverly Tilton ... the girl whose book I told you was published last month, is going to Hollywood to do the movie version and she said I could have her place. She has a nice little dive down there, and I think I could write a lot better."

The older man nodded. "I'll see Devon in the morning. He'll fix you up with a checking account. Go ahead and do what you please but don't forget us."

"I'd never do that and you know it."

"Sure, I know it. I just want you to tell me every now and then."

Borden's eyes filled with tears as he hugged his father briefly and walked rapidly from the room.

They rode slowly down St. Charles Avenue, Favra quiet and still overpowered, unable to think or speak.

"You're in love with me," said Elton Chance, Jr. "Why don't you admit it?"

"Yes, I love you."

He drew her close to him and chuckled. "That's my girl. You just listen to me and we'll get along."

A tiny bell of resentment tinkled in the distance, but was immediately inundated by a wall of passion that seemed to burst inside her like an overripe fruit. His big hand encircled her waist, making it hot and so exquisitely sensitive that she bit her lip.

He carried her up the steps to her apartment with ease, his hands losing no opportunity to seek forbidden places, making the bell ring again but farther away than ever.

He carried her into the bedroom. She closed her eyes and gave herself over to sensation, divining rather than actually knowing what was happening until finally she felt utterly transported, and the touch of him sent such a tide of ecstasy through her that a little cry burst from her lips. Then she lay in deathlike relaxation, a painting of poetic grace.

"Have to go," he was saying as he tied his shoe laces.

"No ... Elt ... no ... please."

"Have to, pet. The world will not wait for the sluggard, you know. Have to complete our bid on the new arsenal in North Mississippi tomorrow. Tell you what ..." He took out a notebook and wrote rapidly. "Here's an address. I'll call the landlord tomorrow and tomorrow afternoon you can move in. Get you out of this pest hole and into a decent place. Costs a hundred a week but you're worth it. Move in tomorrow afternoon and buzz me. When I can get away I'll come out and we'll take up where we left off." He bent over and kissed her quickly.

"So long, kid. Give me a buzz when you get set."

She rolled over, buried her face in her pillow and wept bitterly. The pillow stifled cries that welled from the depths of her soul, cries shaking with pain and disillusionment. Sleep finally claimed her and far into the night occasional spasmodic sobs would shake her. She awoke late the next morning, T'ling celebrating the awakening by presenting her with a steaming cup of coffee. She sat up in bed, her senses dulled and her body sore.

CHAPTER 9
THE ARTS OF LIFE

"WHAT'S THE MATTER, Miss Favra?"

"Nothing, T'ling...run along and drink some coffee."

"There *is* something, too, the matter!"

"There is, of course, but it's my problem that I'll have to fight out myself. Bring me the phone and book. I want to look up Miss Arden's number."

The girl came back presently with the phone, plugged it in a wall socket, handed Favra the book, and taking the empty cup, went out of the room.

"T'ling..." The summons was strident and harsh.

There was a pattering of feet and T'ling came through the door. "Yes'm?"

"What's this address here...on the back of the book?"

She looked and turned red. "I'm sorry I put that there, Miss Favra. It's my friend...you know where you took me that night."

"Do you know his name?"

"Yes'm."

"What is it?"

"Mr. Elton Chansonne."

"Well, T'ling, Mr. Chansonne was here last night with me. Do you know who he is?"

"Well...I guess not..."

Favra was white and trembling with rage. "T'ling, I'm so damn mad I could scream … him and his high and mightiness … Move to this address, he says … buzz me when you get settled …"

She burst into tears again and wept hard for a while then she hurled the cover back and leaped to her feet. "Well, I couldn't have learned any younger."

T'ling stood silently by, her eyes swimming with tears. "I'm sorry I put that address on the book. You know how it is … He called me and I just sort of doodled the address on the …"

Favra hugged the weeping girl. "Shut up," she said slapping her affectionately on a buttock. "It's the best thing you ever did for me. Now come on in here and build me a breakfast and some for yourself at the same time. I want you to eat with me. By hook or crook you seem to be the best friend I have and I love you. I want you to eat with me and I'm going to have my way … Oh, I have to call Arden."

She called Arden who agreed to meet her at the Old Barrel House on Bourbon and from there they would go to Denver Dawson's studio.

Favra ate breakfast, enjoying the manifest discomfort of T'ling who though overjoyed at her mistress' democratic generosity was, nevertheless, embarrassed. Later in the morning Favra took a hot bath, then a cold shower, having come to realize that she was at last beginning to be tough enough to tilt with life and come out without losing too much. In her anger, Elt's attraction had melted like an icicle in a blast of hot air. She climbed out and, in her soaring exuberance, sang a little song under her breath, being interrupted by the doorbell. She put on a robe, went to answer it, and admitted a tall svelte girl with high cheekbones and a glorious mop of flaming hair that would never behave no matter how it was maneuvered.

"I live next door," the girl said, "and I'm leaving. I'm sorry to have been such a terrible neighbor but I've been writing myself into a tizzy and now that it seems I'm a success, I have to leave and I'm asking a favor, if I may."

"Of course," said Favra warmly. "Sit down and tell me."

"Only for a moment." She sat gracefully, but remained poised tensely on the edge of the cushion. "I'm leaving today and a gentleman is coming to pick up my key because he'll live there until I come back. I wonder if you'd mind if I tell him to call here for it?"

"I'd be glad to, and congratulations on the success. May I ask the name of the book?"

"I'll take your address and send you a copy autographed unless you happen to be averse to such nonsense."

"I'd love it." She rose swiftly and wrote the name and address on a slip of paper.

"My name," said the girl putting the slip in her purse, "is Agatha Jones so you'll understand when you see another name on the cover."

"I don't blame you," laughed Favra. "My name is really Favranella McMullin. I certainly wouldn't put it on the cover of a book."

Agatha handed her the key. "He'll call this afternoon ... or when would be the best time?"

"Tell him after six. I'll be home then."

"Miss McMullin, I do appreciate this a lot and again I'm sorry I didn't meet you before but I was just so busy that I didn't even eat properly. I'm fifteen pounds underweight."

"I understand but when you come back a success we must meet again."

"I shall make it a point. Thanks again and goodbye. I've got to be at Moisant Airport in an hour."

T'ling, who had been listening in the background, chuckled and said, "You must've got wool gathers this morning. You didn't even ask her what the man's name is."

"Oh … my goodness. I didn't at that. Well, whoever he is he'll ask for a key and I'll hand it over and that'll be that."

Acy Jones sat like some fantastic buddha behind his counter at the Old Barrel House. His chair was specially made with welded rods to accommodate and support his three hundred and twenty pounds of weight. On one side of the counter was a bowl of peeled boiled eggs and on the other a dish of wheat crackers. No one could ever remember Acy when he was not shoveling eggs into his mouth and washing them down with dark lager.

Favra stepped into the bar and walked over to Acy. "Well, how's my best fellow this afternoon?"

"Better'n usual, Miss Favra; how'n hell are you and where you been these last few weeks?"

"Here and there, Acy. Have you seen a copper-headed siren come in who'd knock your eyes out?"

"Must be her over in the booth. She's tryin' t' git a straight drink down and ain't made it yet. S'matter with her, got sumthin't' fergit?"

"She's trying to get up enough nerve to ask a man to marry her."

"I vow," breathed Acy aghast. "What sorta dope is he, makin' that fine-lookin' hunk o' woman ast *him?*"

"Times change. Will you send me a bourbon and coke over to the table?"

"Sure will, ma'm … Willie …"

"Why the bottled courage, darling?" asked Favra as she sat down.

Arden looked up and smiled weakly. "I'm all worked up, trembly and scared."

"Honey, I'm going to be there."

"I know and I do appreciate it but … Oh, I don't know."

"I do … rearing and background. It just isn't done."

"Oh, it's done all right, but never in the name of art. You know I've been reading up. A lot of artists had mistresses and they painted them nude, lots of them."

"It's a fairly popular pasttime all right, but you needn't go whole hog."

Arden turned pink. "Last night I dreamed I did."

"Well, it was just a dream. Finish that drink and we'll go, as soon as I finish mine. I need one, too."

Dawson's studio was immaculately clean and orderly in a masculine sort of way. It was not richly furnished, but in excellent taste, and the effect was pleasing. He had plenty of comfortable chairs and couches. The room in which he painted was well lighted. In the center of it was a dais arranged ten feet from the easel, covered with a drape of heavy yellow silk.

Dawson was so nervous that he almost ate his cigarette, puffing furiously. "Today I'll take some photographs and study them for position. I'm not too certain how you'd show up best ..." He halted and gnawed his lips, looking appealingly at Favra.

"You can undress behind the screen, Arden," she said helpfully.

Arden's head went up and little knots appeared on her jaws. "I'm being very stupid about this perhaps but if I'm to be nude, what need is there for a screen?" Dawson laughed, delighted, and seemed to relax. "That's a good sign. You're being realistic and if you'll allow me I'll be also. I want to watch you."

Suddenly Favra was not in the room. Arden's heart seemed about to pound through her breast, her skin seemed prickly and alive with a delicious sensation and when she spoke it surprised her. "I *want* you to watch me, Denver."

Favra backed up and effaced herself by sitting behind a canvas stretcher, watching with growing wonder the transformed Arden as she slowly peeled her garments away and stood finally before him, a superb example of beauty, perfect glowing health, and enticing architecture.

Dawson's breath almost whistled while Arden proudly drew her stomach in, thrusting her breasts into prominence, compressing her waist into subtle muscular ridges. She bent one knee and placed upon the dais the other leg stretched straight with the toes resting on the floor. One arm trailed gracefully at her side while the other reached up and grasped the corner of an antique bookcase that formed a background. Favra, impelled by a power beyond her control, stood up, marveling at the natural poise and grace of the girl, the full prominence of her rich breasts now excited and taut, the perfection of the leg with its parallel lines of smooth muscle, the melon smoothness of the other thigh drawn up as she sank down slightly, half sitting, half kneeling, the flawless grace of her small feet, and the glory of her coppery hair.

"Favra," cried Dawson excitedly, "did you see that? She fell into it like … God, who else *could* fall into a pose like that? Hold it, Arden, and I'll take some shots." Shaking with eagerness and excitement Dawson fumbled with his camera and finally made the shot, a second, and a third, then collapsed abruptly on a stool. He lighted a cigarette and waved his long-fingered hand at her. "You can dress now, my dear." His eyes strayed to Favra who still stood in a spell that was expressive and yet full of pain. She could not understand the latter.

In slipping into her clothes Arden managed to be even more graceful than when she removed them. She was transformed now, sure of herself, proud and perfectly conscious of the loveliness of her person and its effect on others. It made a noticeable difference.

"And now," said Dawson, "I'll make drinks for all hands."

He did, serving them in his cozy living room, the walls lined with rich colors of old masters in magnificent reproductions, with here and there a modern or two flaring brightly like a torch from the walls.

"Arden," he said, "if I can capture what you showed on the dais in there a while ago I shall be as famous as Goya—only, of course, I'll never be able to show it."

Arden straightened quickly and stared at him. "And why not, may I ask?"

Dawson's mouth hung open. "Do you mean to tell me you'd agree to let me show it?"

"If you don't show it I shall not pose another time."

Sweat beaded his forehead as he looked at Favra who smiled encouragingly. "I don't think you quite understand, Denver. Arden despises the atmosphere she has been brought up in. She'd like nothing better than to shock her family with just such a thing."

He grasped his glass in both hands as though holding onto a reality that was threatening to escape him. "The hair," he said half to Favra and half to himself. "Over her perfect shoulders, her face with that expression of hauteur, of disdain, of passionate belligerence." He shook his head. "If I can do it ... *if* I can do it!"

With a curious little sound Arden slipped to her knees beside him and placing her arms on his knees said, "Denver, you can do it ... and you *really* think I'm beautiful, don't you?" Her eyes were starry, her damp full lips parted in eagerness and her heart displayed nakedly before him. He touched her face wonderingly, unbelievingly. "Not just beautiful; I don't have just the word, because it isn't something you can weigh or measure. Too much of it comes from within, from your bounding vitality, from your attitude and emotions, from the same thing that made you come to me and give me this opportunity." He shuddered. "I'm afraid ... afraid."

"But why ... why?"

His long fingers touched her face again. "Because nothing less than you on that canvas will be good enough."

"Let's not be foolish," snapped Favra, "and put a standard on the work that no living human being could accomplish, not even Goya."

Arden caught one of his hands in hers. "And I'll be here. Won't that help?"

For a long moment he looked into her eyes. "There may be a body somewhere as good as yours, Arden, but no one else could provide such an inspiration. You are both. If I don't succeed then I deserve to fail."

Back at Favra's apartment Arden stretched on the couch and wriggled sensuously. "How quickly can a person fall in love?"

"Oh … as quickly as you did. Quicker sometimes."

The girl sat up. "Was I that obvious?"

"Not to him maybe, but you were to me. You were absolutely glorious. I can understand better now why Aaron makes such a fetish of beauty. What else is there except seeing and tasting beauty?"

Arden remained silent for awhile. "Make me a promise, Favra."

"What?"

"If I ever get the least bit egotistical will you kick it out of me … hard?"

"Gladly, although Aaron would probably garrote me if he caught me kicking you where people are supposed to be kicked."

"In that you are entirely right," said Aaron walking through the opened door. "I came prepared for one but two adds the unexpected. Why do you want to be kicked, Arden?"

"Because everyone is flattering me and I'm afraid it might go to my head."

"Not as long as you realize the danger. Egocentricity and stupidity are often the same thing. Favra, does the bar run to a drink?"

"Oh, gosh, no. I haven't replenished this week. I'm going to run down to the Barrel House. Acy orders my stuff and I'll bring back a bottle and leave an order."

"Why not phone?" he asked, exercise being anathema to him.

"It won't take over thirty minutes. You two can chat while I'm gone."

She left and Aaron played with a long cigarette for a moment before lighting it. "What will you do with your new freedom, Arden?"

"Live," she breathed ecstatically, "brazenly, dangerously, wonderfully."

"That's a large order for one reared as you must have been."

"I know and that means I'll have to live more dangerously than others. I have so far to go." She sat up, feeling his eyes upon her, somewhat irritated at the throbbing beat of her pulse and the urging of her body. "What do *you* call living?"

"I worship at the cross of beauty. I live it, taste it, rub it into my skin, I immerse myself in it. It can be almost like a palpable medium, like water, ointment, balm. Anything else is sere and mundane."

She looked him over critically. "You feel as you do and yet people would say that you are abnormal."

"And they would be right. As I have told Favra I have learned to live at peace with myself."

"Do you enjoy yourself, I mean, the way you are and everything?"

"Intensely."

"And do you, like most others, find most pleasure in the pleasure of others?"

"Within limits. I find pleasure in beauty transformed. Let us take you for instance. What could I do to make you more beautiful? You hold a tremendous attraction for me. So much, that it's frightening at times."

The drums set up their clamorous thunder and as she swung her legs down from the couch she was conscious that he had looked, watched her, his eyes carefully expressionless. A charge of hot blood made her giddy and she swung her legs back, slower this time, watching his eyes. They followed the movement steadily, lighting up and making her breath come faster. He came and sat beside her, one hand resting on a bare portion of her thigh. "You see you do not resent my hand because you know that I'm not a stallion and there will be no reason for fighting and screaming, and yet you know how deeply I appreciate the texture of your skin and the heat of the life-giving blood that feeds it, the surpassingly excellent structure of you, and the deep quality of your own senses and appreciation."

She felt that she should say something but words could not form over the clamor of her senses, all twittering with surging anxiety, nervousness, and half fledged passion. She was not attracted to him physically, and yet there was a magnetism about him that made her head reel with myriads of half formed possibilities, skittering little birds of fright.

"Stand up, Arden." She did so automatically, as though impelled by some power over which she had no control. His eyes sought hers, caressing, intimate, projecting an almost palpable heat that swept over her like a deluge of some warm sticky fluid, tickling, clinging, and driving her already riotous senses into fresh activity. She tried to think, to shut out the impact of his eyes but his hands had brushed her lightly under the arms, with the touch of an artist spotting a statue with lacquer.

When Favra came in bearing two bottles of whiskey, Arden lay at one end of the couch, her clothes orderly and proper, but the arresting thing was her face. It was as smooth and placid as a pearl, almost ethereal in its complete repose and utter peace that was almost fatigue. Her smile as the other girl came in was quirked at the corners and so cat-like and replete that Favra experienced a pang. Now she *knew*. Arden had had her first lesson.

"Drinks for all?" she asked.

"None for me, Favra," said the girl.

"One for me," said Aaron abstractedly. "A very tall implacable one, asserting undeniable authority."

"I'd better go," said Arden lazily. "They'll be sending out the *gendarmerie* if I'm late for dinner."

"When will you pose again?" asked Favra.

"Whenever he asks me ... tomorrow possibly. I want to see what it is going to look like."

When she had gone Aaron asked, "Pose for whom?"

"I guess you might as well know. Denver is doing a nude of her."

He whistled long and low. "I envy that man."

"I don't know why," she said. "You certainly haven't been letting any grass grow under your feet."

"So you know?"

"Certainly. I listened before I came in then I went around the block slowly."

"Bless you. She was probably the most exquisite thing I ever saw, with no bricks thrown at your dear self. She was magnificent."

"Tell me something. Since I met Elton you haven't ..." She hesitated.

He nodded. "What could I give you now? The gelding must give ground before the stallion."

"Is that why?"

"Of course. I have my pride, you know."

The bell rang stridently.

"A large man," he prophesied. "An impatient man."

She went to the door. "Won't you come in? I suppose you came for the key?"

"Yes." He came in and took a chair. "I'm sorry to put you to this inconvenience."

"No inconvenience at all. Mr. Festival, Mr. er ..."

"Chaisson, Borden Chaisson."

Aaron arose and shook hands. "Thanks," said Aaron with a smile.

"For what?"

"For not breaking my hand. Large muscular men seem to take delight in pulverizing my hand because I am obviously without muscles other than those required for locomotion and performing certain mundane but necessary tasks."

A slow smile showed on Borden's lips. "You're the first ... er, well unmuscular man I ever heard who would admit it. I didn't crush your hand because I have nothing against you and no ego to fatten on your pain."

Favra came back and handed him the key. "Since we're to be neighbors, won't you stay for a drink?"

"Just one," he said stretching his long legs comfortably in front. "I still have my stuff to arrange. My predecessor was a rotten housekeeper." While Favra fixed drinks Aaron examined him critically. He was narrow of hip and his shoulders were so broad that, sitting, they made him seem almost bulky. The illusion was broken when he stood because of his height. His face was rather narrow, his features fine and regular, with a certain wistful thoughtfulness about them.

"A thinker," said Aaron to himself. "A sensitive thinker who is too normal to be bizarre and too artistic to be normal. His lashes are long and his lips just full enough to avoid being severe."

"So you have nothing against me. Maybe you haven't thought about that but many men of your sort would resent me to the point of actual violence."

The smile appeared again. "I don't know what sort of company I find myself in at the present but you at least exhibit a refreshing frankness. I have nothing against you whatever, and it is not because of ignorance. I write and I could not do a convincing job were I not something of a student of a group of men, among whom are Kraft-Ebbing, Ellis, and others. To take offense at a man like you would indicate a certain stupidity, lack of personal introspection and understanding."

Aaron chuckled and lit a cigarette, accepting a drink from Favra. "Something tells me we are going to enjoy our neighbor, Favra. He displays an acuteness and balance that we don't see in quantity."

Her brows contracted. "I keep thinking I've seen you somewhere."

"Doubtless you have. I've been there. By the way, where did you get this superlative bourbon?"

"Acy Jones orders it for me. He runs the Old Barrel House."

"I know Acy. He's a diamond in the rough if there ever was one. He let me sleep off a jag in his place once and pulled the cops out of my hair in order to do it."

He stood up. "I'll have to go now but I'll see you people later if I may."

"By all means," said Aaron affably. "This place is always in a state of chronic open house. Come any time."

Aaron popped his tongue at Favra who was in a brown study, making her start.

"What are you thinking about?"

"I'm trying to remember where I've seen him, but I can't bring it back."

"Personable fellow. Well, I must be going. I'm to have a late dinner with Esta."

"What about her?"

"I'm afraid I don't follow you."

"I've never seen you this interested in anyone. Over this period of time, I mean. You usually take them as they come, then let them go."

"It's very simple, my dear. Where you and most women tolerate me because I'm a novelty, Esta actually enjoys me. Imagine what excellent food for my ego that is."

"Explain that phenomenon if you can."

He stood up and lit a cigarette. "It would be something like an explanation of myself. She is a gourmet and a gourmand at the same time. I do not mind admitting that she is a genius in lots of ways, to wit: she opened doors in one Aaron Festival, the presence of which he has been totally unaware, lo these many years. I seem to have a peculiar streak of normalcy after all."

"When do you have to be at Esta's?"

"At eight."

"It's only seven. I'll run you over. I want to talk."

He resumed his seat. "Talk by all means. This, of course, will have to do with your Friday night appearance at the Chances."

"Yes. I fell in love at first sight with Elt. He's junior and cut from the same bolt as Elton. The resemblance, I found, stopped right there. He brought me home last night."

"Ah…he did? A disappointment, I take it."

"In his attitude. He's cruel, overbearing, his real interest is construction and everything else takes second place or so I believed."

"What made you change your mind?"

"I found out quite by accident that it was he who T'ling was visiting at the Banford Arms. He is a sort of gigolo on call by Esta whenever one of her rich clients feels the need."

"And you consider that reprehensible?"

"I don't think I'm overly prudish but I despise anyone who has a Jekyll and Hyde personality."

"It occurs to me," he observed dryly, "that you are prone to fall in love easily…and out. You haven't said so but I take it that Mr. Chance is not now among your treasury of priceless memories."

"I resent him and I don't like him. If I actively despised him I'd be a little more thoughtful about the whole thing."

"Wisdom of the purest kind. I've come to expect it from you."

"Then you don't think something's wrong with me?"

He laughed. "On the contrary. I think quite the opposite. You're interesting because you are the best example I know of a woman who has been successful in overcoming the mores of her childhood."

CHAPTER 10
TAKING CHANCES

WHEN SHE GOT back Elt was parked in front of the house waiting for her. "What happened?" he asked, frowning as he stepped from the car. "I went to the apartment intending to find you there and it was empty."

"That," she said ironically, "must have been a shock since I am probably the first to ever dare oppose you."

"Most people don't," he said his scowl darkening. "They find it better to play ball with me."

"I refuse to play ball with you and you'd better remember it. I don't come panting everytime *anyone* whistles. That includes you."

"But you said you loved me."

"The more fool I. I did but I'm glad to say you put out the fire quickly enough."

"Look, you might as well know that I don't take no for an answer. I'd never make a go of it in the construction game if I did."

"You'd better get set then, son, because you have in your possession one great big *no*."

He stood leaning easily against his car for awhile then grinned. "Let's have a drink."

"I don't want one."

"You wouldn't send me away thirsty, would you?"

She shrugged wearily. "All right. One drink, but if that is a maneuver to make me change my mind I can save you time. It won't change."

"People's minds change all the time," he said as he followed her up the steps. She opened the door and they went in, with Elt taking the first chair he came to as though it were his own. She made him a drink and sat on the couch.

He tasted it and nodded approvingly. "Now let's get off the firing line, pet, and talk about us. Maybe I was hasty but I can give ground. Come to my place in your own time. I'll even send a van to bring your stuff if you insist. There's plenty of room for it."

Favra puffed on a cigarette and said nothing.

"Okay, then. What is it you want?"

"Me? ... Want? Nothing! Nothing from you, at any rate. It's time your balloon was punctured."

"Not by you, my pet," he said smiling. "I don't give up that easily."

"I don't care about your personal foibles. I'm not coming to your apartment now or ever. Neither on the other hand are you coming here."

"Give me one good reason why."

"Just one?"

"That's all I ask."

"Very well. For one thing when you wanted to meet my maid, T'ling, you'd have to give me an excuse and that would be a bore. When you were called to a certain place to lie abed with some fat dowager you'd have to give an excuse. *That* would be a bore. You asked for one but I'm giving you three. Number three, you haven't mentioned love to me *or* marriage, and if you think you're going to add me to your belt along with the other sordid scalps you have there, you're not only mistaken, you're a complete fool."

His face, gone crimson during her recital, now turned almost purple. "I've beaten women half to death for less than you just said." His voice was hoarse and thick.

"Yes, I had you pegged as a man who would do that, and do you know, if you ever struck me, I'd kill you?"

"I think that would be fun to try."

"Then have at it."

"No, not now. I want to know how you found out about me?"

"That isn't important. What might be important is if your big-shot friends in construction circles knew how you spend your leisure moments."

His face that had been suffused with dark blood now became paler. "I can be dangerous, Favra. Don't push me too far."

"With women, children, and dogs I dare say you're a terror. How many *men* have you ever beaten?"

Again came the rush of blood and he bared his teeth in a mirthless grin. "You have a genius for making me sore."

She stood up. "I'm tiring of it. You may go now."

He got up and with a lunge caught her in his arms, laughing into her upturned face. "I told you I was a rough customer, pet. What say you and I play a little?"

The battle was not long because he was a powerful man and in his hands she was as putty, and at a moment that couldn't have been more critical, the door opened. He turned to look, and in doing so, took his palm from her mouth.

"Please help," she screamed. "... Please ..."

Magically, it seemed his weight came off her and she managed to sit up, just in time to see Borden Chaisson whip a crushing left hook to Elt's jaw. Down he went on a throw rug that skidded him across the polished floor to fetch up with a thump against the wall.

Elt sat up slowly, his eyes pools of greenish light. "Brother of mine, I'm going to kill you for this."

"I kill very easily," said Borden contemptuously.

Brothers... Favra's mind began to clear. Chance, Chaisson, Chansonne. It all became clear now, and she remembered where it was she had seen Borden. It had only been her absorption in Elt that made her forget him. Breath fluttered into her throat as she saw Elt coming up off the floor, enabling her to find her voice. "Kill him, Borden," she screamed. "Tear him apart."

"Ha ha ha," laughed Elt. "That pansy. Why he couldn't fight his way out of a ... !"

Another left hook had snaked out and again the big blond went crashing to the floor. This time he looked up with something akin to hurt surprise. "Brother, you're only making it worse for yourself. Don't you know I was a football player, an athlete, while all you did was stick your nose in books?"

"I know," said Borden coolly blowing on a skinned knuckle. "Trouble is you don't know what *I* did. I'm not going to tell you, either. I am going to make you find out the hard way."

Elt came up from the floor with a rush calculated to pin his brother into a corner and simply brutalize him into submission. As it was Borden ducked easily under the sweeping right that Elt threw and whipped two solid blows, a full-shouldered right and left, to the midsection. For the third time Elton went down, this time holding his stomach and making strange croaking noises trying to regain his breath.

"Why don't you kick him while he's down?" suggested Favra maliciously. "Stomp the very guts out of him."

Borden grinned. "It's a temptation but you see I want that yellow streak of his to come out. I've known it was there for a long time but I never had an opportunity to scare it into the open."

"He told me about the women he had beaten," she said furiously. "Now, Elt..." She walked to where he groveled on his face. "Now let's see how you beat a man. The women offered you no opposition. Get up, you dirty cowardly son-of-a-bitch and get what's coming to you."

"Gee," breathed Borden. "I believe you're sore."

"You saw … didn't you?" she blazed.

"Yes, I saw. Come on, bub; you've been down there a long time. Get up or I'll kick you up as Favra suggested." Elt groaned and struggled to his feet.

"Breathe good, son. I don't want any charges of unfairness."

"I'm going to kill you," snarled the other, saliva drooling from his slack jaw. He made another furious rush and again Borden side-stepped, and stung Elt with a hard left to the eye. Almost immediately it began to swell and turn blue. Elt was more careful this time and managed to get close enough to get in a terrific right that struck the shoulder lifted to meet it but glanced off with enough force to catch Borden under the ear and send him to the floor. With a guttural curse Elt leaped on his brother and sought his throat. Burning, with the unfairness of it Favra poured a full glass of hundred-proof whiskey and, picking her chance, hurled it full in Elt's face, sending him staggering to his feet, choking and blinded.

"Thanks, kid, but I could have handled him all right." He said to his brother, "Get the fumes all cleared out, son. Your tactics do well in a bar room, but if I came down to your level I'd be just the sort of dog you are."

It took some minutes to get free of the effects of the stinging douche of strong whisky which was never intended to be used as an eyewash or an inhalant. Sobbing with rage Elton began a cautious advance that was rendered even more cautious by the fact that his left eye was completely closed now. He swung mightily and rushed suddenly trying to overwhelm his brother and get in a telling blow, but Borden only danced away in a circle and kept flicking out his fist. He was deliberately cutting his brother to bits, refraining from delivering any telling blows, till he chose. Finally with a sob Elt dropped his guard and leaned drunkenly against the wall. Borden bounded in and delivered an openhanded slap with such force that blood spattered the soft tones of the wall but

Elt did not respond. Instead he hung his head and sobbed, tears mixing with blood to trickle down his face.

"I'm blind," he choked. "I can't see a thing."

She could see that this was no less than the truth so she said, "That'll be enough, Borden. Let the sniveling thing be. He might tell papa."

"*I'm* going to have to tell Papa because I have no intention of driving him home. Someone will have to." He dialed a number and listened for half a minute. "Hi, Mom … Borden. Is Pop there?"

He listened for a few seconds. "Sure I'm all right. Just about got the place straight. I'm going to like it fine. Let me speak to Pop … Pop, this is Borden. Now don't let on to Mom but I just had to beat the hell out of Elt." He grinned at the yelp of joy that his father let go. "Yeah … you'd better come out here and bring Grimes to drive him home … Yes, both eyes closed. Okay, bye."

He turned and sat down on the couch. "Chicken, you can have this carpet sent to a cleaner. I'll pay for it."

"Nothing of the sort," she retorted. "I'll pay for it myself and be glad of the chance. I don't know when I've enjoyed anything so much."

Borden accepted a drink and then found a towel which he handed to Elt. "Here, son, you're messing up the place. You'll live, so cut out the blubbering."

Elt raised his head and opening his best eye enough to see, snarled, "I'll kill you, you son …"

Pow! Another terrific slap almost dislocated his neck and would have knocked him down had it not been for the wall.

"Let's keep Mom out of this," said Borden, his voice hard and for the first time angry. "I'd just as soon slap you into a bag of blood and bones." Elt resumed his sobbing, mopping his face and mouth, the lips of which had been shredded by the last slap.

"Pop'll take care of you," he blazed furiously. "You wait and see, you son …" Pow! Again the openhanded wallop. This time Elt sank to the floor and leaned against the wall in impotent misery. Favra, whose enthusiasm had waned now that he was such a thoroughly beaten wreck, began to feel slightly nauseated and took a stiff drink of whiskey chasing it with seltzer.

Twenty minutes later Elton Chance followed by Grimes, the tall colored butler, came through the door that stood open. Chance took one contemptuous glance at the crumpled figure on the floor and turned to Borden. "What happened?"

"Miss McMullin can tell you. I got here in time to save her honor but I don't know what it's all about. I heard the noise of the scuffle and barged in."

"Favra?"

"Well, I'll have to tell you all of it though I'd prefer not. I think I fell in love with Elt but he infuriated me, hurt me, ordered me about like a servant then told me to pack up and go to his apartment in the Banford Arms. I don't operate like that."

Borden's eyes went up at this piece of news and Elton cursed. "I didn't know he had an apartment there."

Favra, in going over the affair, grew angry again. "Then you probably didn't know that he was affiliated with a certain establishment in town that uses men just as some of them use women. In short he was a call boy. I would have never known it if he hadn't been sleeping with my maid whenever he chose, and she inadvertently doodled his address on the phone book. I noticed that it was the same one he gave me. He came here tonight and then, when I told him off, he bragged that he had beaten women half to death for less, then attacked me."

Elt stood up, pointed a shaking finger at her and screamed, "Yes, and I slept with her last night, too."

This time it was his father, and the blow which contained the very thing that Borden had carefully held out of his, bounced the big man off the wall and sent him to the floor, his limbs askew and his head lolling as though the neck was broken.

The father breathed hard and massaged his fist for a moment. "Favra, I can't tell you how sorry I am that this happened. I feel in a way that it's my fault. I should never have let him take you home."

She smiled shakily. "That's all right. I could have come in my car then it would have never happened. It had a flat and that was why I came in a cab."

"Okay, Grimes. Take that towel and beat him into a semblance of consciousness and then steer him to the car. Take him home and call a doctor, but try not to let his mother see him. On second thought … I have a better idea. Take him to Hotel Dieu and tell Dr. Stafford, he's a resident and probably there, that I said to patch him up and on no account let him go for at least three days even if he has to tie him to the bed. There's no need for Elissa to know anything about this."

Elt managed to recover somewhat under Grimes' ministrations, and when he was fully conscious and on his feet his father squared off in front of him.

"Now gather your wits together because you've got a few things to listen to. You're going to the hospital to keep your mother from knowing what happened. If she finds out, I'll know where from, and it'll be rough on you. I'm not kicking you out of the company as I'd like to because you are useful to me. I don't think you'll leave on your own because of the salary you draw, but just one more escapade like this and you'll duck out for Alaska or some place and love it. Now, Grimes, get him out."

They had gone, Grimes, Elt, and his father, but Borden sat on the couch rolling a highball between his palms, frowning at the floor.

"If you're thinking about what Elt said … about us, I mean, he told the truth. I won't start this acquaintance by trying to lie to you."

He shook his head. "No, it wasn't that. Things like this make me ill. You're fine and honest. You fell in love with him because he looked like Pop. A girl who wouldn't fall in love with Pop is a fool. If you had slept with me, Elt would have held it against you but turned around it's different. I'm a charter member of the Live and Let Live Club. What you choose to do with whom is your own affair. Naturally, you didn't show the best taste in picking my ever-loving brother, but I can understand why."

Favra was aware that she was undergoing a remarkable change listening to him. She found herself studying his sensitive face, the length of his dark silky lashes and the sculptured column of his neck, the muscles of which flashed into tautness when he moved his head, a head of almost leonine cast with its tumbled profusion of black curls.

So rapt was her study that the silence had lasted for several minutes before she snapped suddenly back to her surroundings.

"Something tells me," he said laughing, "that I've been through a mental mill."

The furious flush that mounted to her cheeks was evidence enough. For a moment she held her breath in embarrassment then laughed with him. "Okay, you caught on. I was wondering why I could have forgotten you."

"That's easy to explain. You never actually saw me because you were stunned by Elt's overpowering personality."

For a moment she said nothing, then she tilted her head slowly and began to weep silently. He came and sat beside her putting an arm about her shoulders in a brotherly fashion. "I didn't mean to make you cry. Please forgive me."

She raised her head abruptly forgetting her tears. "I will not. You just said something very nice about me and I will not forgive you ... you *meant* it. There was no frivolity in your voice and it made me all weak and soft inside. I'm sorry I cried."

"No need to be," he said brightly. "You're more beautiful than ever when you cry. Gotta go now, chicken. Still got a lot of straightening up to do."

For a long time after he left she lay on the white couch trying to force her mind into order. Borden's face, very definitely etched in her memory now, kept inserting itself into her thoughts throwing them awry again. Finally with a toss of her head she went to bed.

CHAPTER 11

CONSUMMATION DEVOUTLY WISHED

A T BREAKFAST the next morning Alice was absent and Favra felt concerned. "What do you suppose has happened to her?"

"I don't know, my dear, but immediately we finish our repast I shall seek out the hovel in which she lives and see. Her absence worries me."

Favra pulled a hot doughnut in half and inhaled the fragrant steam, turning a problem over in her mind. "Professor, are you a good actor?"

"Oh … average, I'd say. Why?"

"Because it is in my mind to tell you something. But if you botched the follow-through everything would be ruined and I'd lose a good friend."

"I think under those conditions I'd be an excellent actor."

She pondered for a moment longer then nodded. "I'm going to do it and I must insist that you keep your wits about you because what I shall say will shock you. You *must* not give me away!"

"I shall do my mortal best, my dear. I give you my word."

In another man that phrase would have sounded pompous but she knew that he had not used it idly.

"Professor, Alice is not Alice at all. She is Antoinette Dumaire."

The old man clutched the table with both hands and went as pale as death, his throat working spasmodically. Jesse, coming

8

to the table with fresh coffee, noticed his condition. "Geez, Prof, what's the matter with you?"

"Get some brandy or something quick, Jesse."

"Yes, ma'm…"

He dashed away and came back with a glass and half a pint of cheap whiskey. He poured a stiff drink and pressed it on the old man. "Here, Prof, drink this down and it'll bring you back."

The Professor, his hands trembling violently, managed to get the drink down, breathed deeply and nodded, the suggestion of a smile showing on his pallid lips. "Thank you. I shall be fine in a moment."

"I should have been more tactful," said Favra contritely. "I just didn't know."

His smile was wan. "That is because I stay behind my cloak so religiously that no one knows me. It is not always a good idea."

"Now," she said leaning forward earnestly. "It is up to you to *discover* it. You began to suspect the night you took her to Tujacques and it has grown."

"Trust me, my dear. This means too much to make a miscue. How did you know?"

"She told me and…" She stopped abruptly. She had almost told him where his little monthly stipend had come from, but she caught herself just in time. The blow, she feared, would be too much for his pride.

"She told me," she began again, "just as you did. And, Professor…"

"Yes, my dear?"

"Please don't be a fool. Discover her and marry her. Naturally you can't call back your youth but you can give each other the remaining years of your lives."

"To be a fool at my age," he sighed, "is to admit that life has taught me nothing. May we expect you to stand at our modest nuptials?"

"I'd better be there," she said warningly. "It couldn't go off right without me."

He nodded, his eyes moist and his lips trembling. "Again I must repeat my futile words...how I thank God for you, Favra McMullin. How I wish I could return some of your kindness."

Her hand closed gently over his. "We're friends. We mustn't talk about returning favors. Now run along and see Alice and...good luck."

As she walked back to the apartment she felt amazingly happy and light in spirit. Ever since she was a child it had always made her feel buoyant when she did a kindness for someone.

T'ling met her at the door, her eyes anxious. "What happened here last night? The place is all bloodied up. I was just about to call the police."

"Your precious Mr. Chansonne got the hell beaten out of him."

T'ling hung her head. "I sure am sorry about him. I didn't know he was that kind of man, but he is so big. Who beat him?"

"The man who took Agatha Jones' apartment. I didn't remember him but he's Chansonne's brother, only Elt isn't Chansonne and Borden isn't Chaisson—their name is Chance. Now you run along and forget the whole thing except you can take some cold water and see if you can get the blood off the wall. I'll send the carpet to the cleaners."

A telephone call from Arden cut into further conversation. She was so excited that Favra felt its intense reflection, became excited also. "I was going this morning and when Leslie tried to make me tell him where, I cut him dead and told him I'd tell the whole story of the other night to Mother and Father if he so much as raised his voice to me. He slunk off and didn't say another word. I'm so happy this morning I can hardly stand still. Do you suppose Denver has the picture developed?"

"I'm sure he has. I know I couldn't sit around knowing it was there to be developed and do nothing...Oh, yes. I'm sure he has, because he develops his own negatives. You'll be able to see about a sixteen by twenty print of it I'm sure."

"I'm going alone and I'm not the least afraid. I don't even need you anymore unless you just want to come along. I'd love to have you but what I mean is I'm not afraid anymore. Isn't it wonderful?"

Favra let go a peal of laughter. "Honey, everything in the world is wonderful to you right now, and for that matter, me too. I had an experience last night that I'll not forget for many a year but it came out all right."

"Oh, you did? Tell me about it."

"Some other time, dear, when we're together. It'll take too long."

"I want to share your troubles because you have been so wonderful to me. I want to help."

"Tell me something; how do you feel about last night?"

Arden was silent for a moment. "It's hard to explain but … Hell, I'm not going to be goody-goody about it. It stunned me and I haven't recovered yet. I had no idea it could be like that and yet there's something …" She paused.

"Something lacking?"

"Yes. I've never had an experience like that and my nerves are still dead from the shock but …"

"I know, dear. You'll find out … later."

"When will I see you?"

"Oh … you can come by after your sitting or I'll drop by Denver's. Whichever happens first."

"Okay … see you."

Favra accepted a cup of coffee from T'ling and, while she drank it, thought about a statement of Aaron's that Denver would not be able to paint Arden. The electric impact of her glorious body before him would throw a psychological block into his creativeness. She sipped her coffee wondering about it, thought she would go to the studio, decided against it and ended up by slipping on a pair of cream flannel slacks, red and white T-shirt. To T'ling she said, "I'm going out and I don't know when I'll be back. I'll just have a cold lunch when I come in."

"Yes'm, I'll fix it for you and put it in the ice box. Can I call the cleaners about the carpet? I think they have something that they can roll over it. Something that puts out suds then sucks them back up."

"Call them and see. I hope they can clean it without taking it up."

When Denver let Arden into the studio that morning he seemed nervous and distraught but so was she. "Did you develop the picture?"

"Yes, it's perfect. I've even sketched the outlines."

"May I see it?"

"Certainly … in here."

He lifted a huge print from a table and handed it to her. "Oh … my!" The picture was more revealing than she had imagined and a faint flush came to her cheeks. "I had no idea it would be that good," he said. "What appears to be a good shot sometimes doesn't come out that way on the print."

"Then … it's good?"

He laughed. "Look at it. Could it be any better?"

She smiled up at him. "Not if you say it couldn't. What shall we do this morning?"

He turned away and began rearranging things, paint pots, charcoal, drawing paper, manifestly flustered. "This morning," he said without turning around, "we'll do some contours, fill ins; I'll want to make sure my anatomy in the sketch is absolutely perfect. If it isn't, then it won't cook. This is one thing I will not half do."

"Denver, you won't half do it. I know you won't."

"Very well," he said avoiding her eyes. "Will you take the position, the original position? Take it precisely as you did before,

or as near that as possible." He kept puttering and avoiding looking at her till she had unzipped her dress and was ready to take it
off, then she stopped.

"Denver."

He turned cautiously. "Yes?"

"Please watch me." There was a richness in her voice that
seemed to constrict his throat but he watched as she went
through her poetic routine of undressing, then assumed her old
position. The muscles near his shoulder blades ached, his palms
were dank with sweat, which also beaded his forehead. His hands
and arms were as unwieldy as sticks as he picked up his charcoal and dashed off several experimental strokes. He stopped,
dropped the charcoal with a gesture of distaste.

"What's the matter?"

His eyes were dull with despair. "I'm doing it all wrong;
it doesn't come out right..." He erased what he had done and
started over. Again he stopped, crumpled the sketch and threw
it away. Quickly he set another sheet in place and, with his face
tense, wet, and cut with lines of effort he dashed off a sketch with
unbelievable speed. He stepped back, looked it over and shook
his head. "It's no use. I simply can't. I can't, that's all. You might
as well put on your clothes."

"Look at me, please."

He looked, unwillingly, his face tortured with the bitterness
of failure undershot with a pain that had nothing to do with failure. His eyes had the dumb animal glaze of a sick dog, miserable,
begging, and fixed.

"Come here ... please."

A hand fluttered up in protest, trembled and fell at his side
again. "No! I can't come there. ... I couldn't stand it. I can't stand
it ... For God's sake put your clothes on. Do you want to drive me
mad? Put them on, do you hear?"

The frenzy died under the warmth of her steady gaze and
something like a sob racked his throat.

"Come here, Denver." Her voice was still soft and infinitely tender but it bore undertones of steel, of command. He caught his hands together and wrung them in confused desperation.

"Please don't ask me to come there. Don't make me do it. My God, can't you see ..."

"I said come here." This time there was no mistaking the command and he started toward her, his feet dragging trance-like, his eyes begging her to release him from her spell. As he approached, she pointed to her feet where the dais stood on a little raised platform covered with the magnificent spread of yellow silk. "Sit down."

He sat slowly his eyes fastened on her as she leaned upon the dais, a lush figure done by the master of all sculptors and painters, in rose, white shading subtly into tan, and in her eyes he saw something he had never seen there before. They worked on his consciousness hypnotically, growing abnormally large to him till they seemed to flow toward and engulf him.

Slowly she let herself down from her position, then the softness and warmth of her body came against him, her arms about his neck, the overpowering sweetness of her clean person, the faint elusive fragrance of her hair that seemed to smother him, sending his mind into a cataleptic paralysis.

Her lips came away from his, trembling, damp, shining through the darkening cloud of her hair, parted to allow the inrush of air, her tongue quivering from its recent efforts. He pulled her roughly to him a groan of mingled emotions squeezing itself from between his teeth.

"Arden, you shouldn't have done it ... you shouldn't."

She pushed his head back and looked directly into his eyes. "I had to ... Don't you think I felt it, too? Don't you know by now that I love you?"

"You ... love me?"

A little gurgle like laughter bubbled in her throat. "Oh ... you utter fool ..."

All the starvation of years, the defeats, frustrations, thwarted efforts, women who sneered at him, critics who had called him a machine, a draughtsman, foamed up in his chest and were released through a flood of bitter masculine tears, his face buried in the cool surface of her flesh, her hands back of his head caressing him as they would a hurt child.

Favra had let herself in and hearing nothing walked quietly through the house coming on the scene just as Dawson had cast his charcoal down in disgust. She had stopped suddenly and hidden by a curtain watched with fascination the birth of a woman and the rebirth of a man. Trembling, her throat aching with the poignancy of Arden's victory, she walked blindly back to the street and toward her house.

CHAPTER 12
SELF DISCOVERIES

THAT AFTERNOON she received a call from the Professor. "I thought that you would like to know, my dear. Alice, Toni I shall henceforth call her as of old, has something bordering on pneumonia. I finally found her ten minutes ago so I dashed out right away and called an ambulance. Then I called you."

"Where are you taking her?"

"To Charity of course."

"If you do I'll hate you the rest of your life. You take her to Touro and get a private room for her. Ask for Dr. Bailey and tell him I sent her and I want the very best medical care that money can buy. Do you hear me, Professor?"

"Er ... yes, I hear you, but ..."

"Don't but me. You do just as I say and I'll be there when she arrives. I'll have everything ready when you get there. Goodbye."

Alice had been admitted, found to be not as ill as the Professor had thought and now Favra was talking to him in the corridor. "Why don't you go home and get some rest, Professor? This has been a strain on you. I'll stay and let you know if anything happens."

"Oh, no ... no, indeed. I'll stay right here. You see, she doesn't know I know who she is yet. I couldn't leave now. You go ahead and I'll call you. There's no need for both of us to stay."

"Very well. I'll go talk to Dr. Bailey. He's an old friend."

In the doctor's office she took a seat and a cigarette. As he lit it for her, the slanting sun cast a beam of ruddy light across his severely aquiline face, strong, kind and wise.

"It was very kind of you to look out for an old beggar woman."

"That old woman has eaten breakfast with me almost every morning for a year. She's my friend and I'm sure she isn't a beggar by choice."

He smiled gently. "Always the same, aren't you? I don't suppose you'd reconsider and marry me."

"No, Frank. You wouldn't want to marry me if you knew me well. I'm not your sort."

"What sort is that?"

"Oh, you know; steady housewife sort. Salt of the earth and right down the line according to the rules."

"Still no rules for Favra?"

"Still my own rules for Favra. I'm afraid you'd never understand."

"That's not why you won't marry me though. I take out your appendix, fall in love with you and I think I've seen you five times since."

"Would you rather I kidded you along?"

"No, I'd rather you married me."

"It wouldn't work, I've told you that. A husband for me amounts to more than it does for many women. I couldn't honestly ask you to take time from your profession to devote to me and yet that's what I'd have to do in order not to feel left out of things."

He sighed. "Well, I tried again and I'll try yet again. I still think you're the most wonderful person in the world."

"That's another reason against it. I'm not and I couldn't bear to have you find out that I had let you down."

He tried to smile brightly but failed at it. "Frustration in love has been said to produce genius. I should go down in the annals of medicine with great honor."

⚜ ⚜ ⚜

Back in her apartment she paced the floor, a bundle of nerves. There was no word from Arden and she wasn't at home. A call to Dawson's apartment produced no results even though she let the phone ring for ten minutes. She watched the phone, wondering if the Professor would call, wondering if Arden was in trouble. Aaron, followed by Borden, came in and she almost kissed them from relief.

"Am I glad to see you two mugs," she said excitedly. "I was about to work up a case of nerves."

"I can never resist being overjoyed when I'm made unaffectedly welcome," said Aaron as he arranged himself comfortably on the couch. "However, that word 'mugs' coming from your lips jarred my highly tuned sensibilities."

"From her lips," said Borden leaping into the breach, "it sounded positively elegant, like *compadres* or *mes amis*. Transmuting lead into gold is no trick for her."

"Goodness … what about drinks after all those bouquets?"

They both nodded acceptance while Aaron turned to Borden. "My good fellow, you are free to enjoy our hospitality, drink our liquor, but please remember that I am the one who produces the bullet-like back chat."

"As you have seen," she said, laughing as she poured drinks, "anyone who sleeps late is lost in Borden's company. By the way, how is your brother?"

"My brother is licking his wounds I suppose. I haven't bothered to find out."

"I'm just morbid enough to have wanted to be ringside at that slaughter," said Aaron with an admiring glance. "I hear you dispatched him with finesse."

Borden shrugged. "He's as clumsy as an ox. He was a fair tackle at the University but he couldn't hit me if I was tied."

"I'm worried about Arden," she put in, handing drinks around.

"I can't think of anyone I'd be less worried about," observed Aaron.

"She's not home, she's not at Denver's … there's no one there, and I'm uneasy. I got her into this section and I don't want anything to happen to her."

"I thought that was why you brought her into the Quarter."

"Oh, hush … you know what I mean."

"There are times," said Aaron in mock fright, "when rapier repartee is contraindicated."

"Where's Esta tonight?" Favra asked.

"Esta is in the bowels of her inimitable dungeon whipping jaded gonads into a frenzy."

Borden smiled with a touch of slyness. "I was there once, if you mean the place I think you mean. The Madam is a striking brunette who seems to look through you."

"The same," said Aaron. "I have conceived a great affection for her."

Borden eyed him closely. "Er … will you go over that again?"

Aaron's laugh was joyous. "That's one thing you didn't know about me, is it? I, friend Chance, unless you insist on Chaisson, am what you might class as a double negative. In some fields that makes a positive. In my particular case I should say it would mean that I'm twice as negative as I appear."

Borden lit a cigarette and blew two perfect rings. "Aaron, you drive a hard enigma. If you will answer one question I will then be lost for good should it be answered in the negative. Were you ever in love with a man?"

The other shuddered earnestly. "My good fellow, you insult my esthetics. By what stretch of imagination could you class a man as beautiful? No, Borden, I shall have to confuse you further. I have never been in love with a man."

"What do you call yourself?"

"As I said, a double negative. There have been some men whom I have offended by being alive but they are not many. I find that odd because there are males whose gender is not nearly as foggy as my own and who are actually afraid to associate with your rugged type because I have seen men fly into unreasoning rages at the very sight of them."

Borden sucked on his cigarette with relish. "That is explicable. A very masculine man, no matter how much hair he might have on his chest, has latent homosexual tendencies. Some strong, some weak, most of them subconscious. It is this subconscious awareness that makes them see in this type of individual a reflection of themselves. It is strong enough to create a fear and the object of fear is generally hated. No one could tell you why."

"I'm going to fix more drinks," said Favra. "I seem to be left out of this esoteric conversation although I'm enjoying it immensely. Answer the doorbell, will you, Aaron?"

He opened the door and admitted Leslie Drake whose face was seamed with angry determination.

"Where is my sister?" he asked, ignoring the men and walking across the room to the little bar where Favra stood with a whiskey bottle in her hand.

"I'm sure I don't know. She hasn't been here today."

"She's not home."

"Then we can safely assume that she is some other place."

"You will please not be sarcastic ... you ..."

"Er ... pardon me, son," said Borden in a soft voice, "but if you have any diatribe up your sleeve I'd advise you to save it."

Leslie turned about. "Sir, do you know this ... this woman?"

"I'm very well acquainted with her."

"Then you will understand me when I say that to me she is common, low, vulgar, and for all I know her body is for hire."

Borden came to his feet with catlike ease and Aaron, perching on the edge of his chair, almost yelped with joy.

"You will understand me," said the former, "when I say that you, in one fell swoop, overtalked yourself." He seized Leslie by the shirt front and, backing him against the wall, slapped him with such gusto that his eyes crossed alarmingly. The return slap, bringing into play the bony side of the hand along with the knuckles, was even less kind, leaving the hapless Leslie with a head full of ringing bells and a face that had suddenly grown tight and lopsided.

"That's enough," said Favra putting her hand on Borden's arm. "Leslie, I do not know where Arden is. I haven't seen her all day. If she's not home then I suppose it's because she didn't want to go home."

Leslie, humiliated, his face feeling as though he had been debating unsuccessfully with a horde of hornets, stumbled out of the apartment and down the steps.

"I'm going to call Denver's place again," she said, but again she could get no answer.

"Why don't you call the marriage license bureau?" asked Aaron idly, somewhat disappointed that the anticipated slaughter had ended so quickly.

"Oh … do you suppose they did …? But I can't call them at this time of night."

"Worry no more, Favra. You've been carrying a load. You are trying to do too much for too many people. The beggar woman for instance. What hospital did you take her to?"

"How did you know that?"

He shrugged. "I walk along Royal, Burgundy, Liberty, Conti, Toulouse … I see many things. I see you dash out when I'm coming to get a drink. I see an ambulance a few minutes later pull away from a bedraggled place not a block from here with Alice aboard. Ergo, you are hurrying up to see that she is taken care of … simple."

She shook her head and handed drinks around. "I'm glad it's that simple. I thought you were going into one of your mind-reading acts again."

"You flatter my poor penetration," he said with a chuckle. "I spit on mind readers."

For the next four days she divided her time between the hospital and answering questions. The police asked her questions, private detectives asked her questions. Leslie called and asked questions, becoming insulting since there was no danger of reprisal over the phone. Mr. Drake called and asked questions, and on it went till she was ready to scream. Night had fallen and she was alone and after the third phone call she banged the receiver down and marched out of her apartment.

At her knock Borden opened his door. "Well, this is a pleasure. I was trying to root out a touch of inspiration for my fifth chapter. You're it. What'll you drink?"

She sat with a bounce on a dun leather couch, her brow furrowed and her eyes furious. "A double bourbon with seltzer on the side. I'm burned up. You'd think *I* had kidnapped Arden the way people carry on. I'm getting damn sick and tired of it."

He came back with her drink and falling to his knees, placed his elbows on hers and gazed into her eyes. "You're tired, kid. Tell Uncle Borden about it."

"Well, the police have been heckling me, then private detectives, then the family. I'm as anxious to find her as they are and dammit I'm sick of them yammering at me." She put down her drink on a glass-topped coffee table and covering her face with her hands began to sob softly. He sat beside her and held her close like a parent soothing a child. "Cry it out. You'll feel better."

She clung to him sobbing harder till at last it ceased except for an occasional spasmodic contraction of her throat. She raised her head and attempted to smile, but it didn't quite come off, the corners of her mouth quivering and turning Borden's insides to jelly. Without thinking, his lips closed over hers and with a tired fluttering sigh she gave in and let herself be drawn to him as pliant as a reed, unresisting, soft, and so delightful to hold that his emotions scattered like wild sheep, sending a feeling of drunkenness to his head. Suddenly he broke away and stood up. "Now, what in the hell did I have to go do that for?"

Favra, no less moved and even more surprised, leaned back against the couch and fought to quell her racing thoughts, her heart beating out a song of wild happiness. There had never been anything like this … never in all her life.

His words, however, made her strike back. "I'm sorry," she said. "I didn't know it'd do that to you. I'll go home now."

He whirled about. "Oh, for Christ's sake, don't say that, and you're not going home." He walked back and faced her, his intense face dark with the power of some tumultuous emotion. "Look, I'm sorry I said that. Will you forgive me?"

She could not keep up the pretense any longer and her arms went out to him. "No … not unless you kiss me again."

He bit his lip for a moment, then with a quick swoop he caught her under the arms and pulled her erect. He did not kiss her immediately, but gazed into her eyes with a longing and hunger that she had never before seen in a man's eyes. He's been hurt, she thought, bitterly hurt, and he's afraid. He thinks he might get hurt again. He's deep and sensitive … Oh, Borden, I'll never hurt you, never as long as I live … can't you see that in my eyes … the way you're looking into them …. Evidently he could, because when he kissed her it was gentle, sweet and so tender that tears came to her eyes again. This is Elton … not the other … Borden received his father's qualities, gentleness, consideration, thoughtfulness. Oh, Borden, why has it been so long?

He drew away and passed his hand over the tawny silken masses of her hair in a caress that hurt her throat, making her rub her cheek against his powerful forearm and kiss it in gratitude and thankfulness not untinged with humility.

She turned her head. "Do you hear someone knocking?"

He listened. "It's not here—it must be … maybe it's at your place. Shall we see?"

She nodded and they left his apartment holding hands like schoolmates. "It's two people," she said. "Why, it's … *Arden* … Darling, where have you been?"

"Oh, Favra …" The girl rushed into her arms, her eyes sparkling like gems, wet with tears of joy.

"What say we go inside for the kudos?" drawled Borden practically. "They seem in order."

Inside, Favra looked at the most radiant person she had ever seen. Arden was simply beside herself with joy and Denver, his face flushed, seemed more alive than she had ever seen him. Gone was the bitter twist to his mouth, the cynical glint in his deep eyes. Tonight he seemed almost boyish. Favra hugged the girl, she hugged Denver then both of them at the same time. She whirled around. "Oh … forgive me but I'm not thinking tonight. Arden Drake and Denver Dawson, may I present Mr. Chance, Borden Chance."

Polite things were said till the amenities were taken care of, then Arden spun around and catching Favra by the arm said, "Did I hear you call me Arden Drake?"

"Well … I, yes … Ohhhh. Don't tell me … *you've done it!*"

Denver's face grew redder and his grin threatened to get out of bounds.

"You're thick tonight," murmured Borden laughing. "You should have seen that at first sight."

"I was too glad to see her. Do you know that your family has had every cop in New Orleans, private and public, looking for you?"

Arden laughed delightedly. "Goody. I'm glad to death. It'll shake them out of that smug musty atmosphere they've been in for so long … Favra, can't we have a drink?"

"Of course. Borden, will you fix them? I want to hear all about this."

"Well," Arden began, "Denver was so upset that second day that he couldn't paint…" The Dawsons vied for the reddest face but Arden shook her head and plunged on. "And I knew why…so…" She laughed and put her palms to her face. "I fixed it and then Denver insisted on making an honest woman of me. Now…and you won't believe this…the painting is *finished;* he did it all in the past four days and, Favra…I never looked like that in my life. You won't believe it."

"I'm going to do yours the easy way," said Denver finally finding his voice. "I'll take the photo, blow it up on sensitized canvas and then paint over it."

"Just so I get one," she said. "Don't forget that."

"I won't and you know something else…I think I can paint now. I mean things for myself. I have something I think will knock your eyes out. I'm going to try it as soon as we get settled."

"But where have you been? I've been trying along with a thousand other people to find you."

Arden answered. "We went over to Grande Isle. It was marvelous…Oh, Favra, I'm so happy and you did it all. You got me out of that house, you introduced me to Denver and you made me pose for him."

"Oh, hush. You both had the ingredients—all I did was mix well."

"Er…" Borden cleared his throat. "If you don't mind, folks, the drinks."

Drinks were consumed and plans made for the unveiling of the picture at Denver's apartment in three days, which time would be spent by Favra and Arden putting the place in feminine order, cleaning and making a general stir.

"You had better come stay with me," put in Borden. "In that hen's nest, you'll be as much in place as a pair of dice at a church social."

"He will not," said Arden… "We'll have plenty for him to do."

Denver groaned. "That's what I was afraid of. Genius aborning and they are going to thrust a feather duster in his hands."

They had gone, but Favra still paced the floor with a drink in her hand.

"Sit down, or you'll work up a case of nerves. What's bothering you now?"

"I don't know. I suppose I've been going too hard." She stopped pacing and faced him. "Borden, how'll I manage to get the Professor and Alice to take money from me so they can live decently? Fate has handled them so badly that I want to see that they can live the rest of their lives in comfort."

"You have a lawyer, don't you?"

"Yes, in Houston. He takes care of my business in the Lincoln oil fields. I have another in Dallas."

"Good men, I suppose?"

"The best … why?"

"Why not call them and explain what you want to do, in what amount and just have them mail it in to the address you give them? They can divert it from your regular dividends, and then you can claim them as total dependents and take it off your income tax."

Her eyes lighted. "That's perfect, Borden. I could tell Stafford or Fleming to do it anonymously every month and they'd never catch on."

"That's right, or just tell them to hold their tongues if questions arise from here."

"I'll do it tomorrow." She sat beside him. "Now that's off my mind I can breathe freely."

They sat for some time wrapped in their own thoughts till at last she felt the touch of his hand on her back. She allowed him to hold her close and with the rising thud of her heart she lifted her face for his kiss. Swiftly, powerfully he lifted her across his lap and cradled her in the crook of his left arm, giving her a long searching look.

Her lips quivered involuntarily as she spoke from the depths. "Borden, I'll never hurt you."

She could feel his muscles grow taut. "Now who's mind reading? How did you know what I was thinking?"

"Because of your reaction when you kissed me for the first time."

He nodded. "That's right, but you just said something that just saying won't quite get."

"I think I know what you mean, but do you realize that you haven't said anything to me?"

Again he nodded. "Yes. I suppose I'm expecting too much. The way I got burned has made me afraid even of a picture of fire."

"Borden, would you hurt me?"

"Not if it were humanly possible to avoid it."

"It is."

"How?"

"Love me."

His breath hissed as he inhaled sharply, then he laughed. "Aren't we the careful ones!"

"*Borden, love me!*" In that one sentence she put all the hurt, the longing, and the resentment against fate that she had ever suffered. Her breast labored and tears stung her eyes.

"I can't … I'm afraid … I …"

She sat up straight "Afraid of what … are you a coward?"

His face paled. "I don't know. I guess so …"

"Kiss me."

"No, I'd better not …"

With a little cry of anger and despair she pulled herself to him, her lips avidly seeking his, thrilling to the sudden upsurge of muscular reaction and the hungry attack of his mouth. When she finally lifted her head he seemed staggered, weak, but still fearful, still unsure of himself.

"Oh, Borden, what can I do?"

"God, I don't know. You can get up and let me go home."

She leaped to her feet and ran rapidly to the door, locked it, and then went to her bedroom where she hid the key, stripped her clothes from her body and put on a web thin nylon housecoat that covered her in a cloud of smoky blue fabric. She came back to the couch and stood for a moment before him, watching the sweat glisten on his forehead and his hands clench spasmodically.

"Please don't, Favra. I..."

Again her lips covered his, the fragile fabric billowing excitingly, fragrantly about them. She could feel the clutch of his arms through the housecoat, skidding along her sensitive skin as though she had nothing on, heard the moan he could not contain, felt the spasmodic movements of his tortured body.

He pushed her away and stood up. "Favra..." His voice was breathless and hoarse. "How much of this do you think I can stand?"

She stood up, too, her sharp-tipped breasts making delightful tents in the garment. "Why stand it... can't you see at all... at all?"

She tossed her disheveled hair back with an angry motion of her head and with a single sinuous motion shrugged out of the garment standing before him, her skin pinkly translucent, luminous, smooth as a new pearl. Borden stood transfixed for a moment then with a low sound coming from his throat caught her in his arms with such force that the breath left her. Her ribs ached, but again the song of victory rose in her heart, and the taste of blood where her lips were cut from the force of his kiss was like a rare brandy.

In the hour that passed swiftly there was no time to move to a better place but since the carpet had been cleaned it was soft, fluffy, and comfortable. Her head was pillowed on his shoulder and her skin acutely aware of the hot damp touch of his, the conditioned muscles of his side and the weight of a leg that still possessed her.

Her mouth moved to his for a moment then away to his ear. "Couldn't you see how I loved you, you fearful man?" A wave of almost unendurable emotion swept her and she clung to him hard, then sighed and relaxed again.

"I guess I could ... but I was afraid."

"Are you afraid now?"

"No, I'm not afraid now. Somehow this has made me know you so much better. I feel I've known you all my life."

CHAPTER 13
A PUBLIC UNVEILING

THE PARTY at Denver's apartment was large. In addition to the French Quarter habitues, there were Mr. and Mrs. Chance, Mr. and Mrs. Drake and Leslie who had come prepared to resent anything they saw, and in truth did not know why they had been asked because Arden had been candidly blunt with them. To their threat of civil action she reminded them that she was of legal age, and there was nothing they could do about it but if they would like the surprise of their lives they could visit her on Saturday night when there was to be a party and an unveiling. Of what, she neglected to say. There were Aaron and Esta, Lofton Kramm looking aloof and superior, Linda DeForest who managed to stay out of any groups that included Favra and, since Ecco Tying was there and also avoiding Favra, they were thrown together a lot. Ecco had recovered but his voice was still not his own and it had been said that he was secretly pleased with the new hoarse note.

There had been drinks and much circulating, with the Chances drawing attention due to their social standing, and having the time of their lives. Elton could hardly keep his eyes off Arden, a fact which Favra noted, and it amused her without stirring jealousy. She was elated because of it as it was the first concrete evidence that Elton had not left too much of a scar.

Denver Dawson stood up on a chair and addressed his guests. "Ladies and gentlemen, this is a party with a double purpose. First, to show off my wife, and the other to unveil a painting. It is *not* a copy of anything else that has ever been done before. This is my own, although when you see it you will agree with me that I was merely the medium through which a beauty never before equalled has been preserved on canvas." He reached over and with a deft snatch yanked the drape of yellow silk from the picture. Dead, utter silence fell upon the room, a silence that seemed thick and sticky.

Favra was so raptly engrossed that she forgot to watch faces, so she never saw the deathlike pallor of Mr. and Mrs. Drake or the horror registered by Leslie.

Aaron Festival was the first to recover his voice. Like an automaton he walked across the intervening space, a look of curious purpose on his face. "Dawson, you have scooped the universe. This thing is not merely beautiful, it is positively fabulous."

A storm of noise arose that carried a scattering of applause, several loud voices, a whistle and other evidences of incredulous enthusiasm.

"I wonder why the Professor doesn't come," Favra whispered to Borden.

"Is he supposed to come?"

"Yes, he's going to be a great art critic tonight."

"You," said Borden, his eyes brimming with admiration, "are the damnedest she-devil…"

Elton Chance, who could look at the picture without having to worry about who noticed him, was drinking his fill. "Shades of Paradise," he murmured.

"She is lovely, isn't she?" said Favra as she approached and slipped a hand in his. He clutched it without looking at her.

"Oh… of course. What I'm speaking of is that any man who could capture what he has in a mere painting simply isn't real. It's done with mirrors or something. Look at the color, the tones, the sheen of her hair and the expression on her face. It should be named 'Passion at Bay.' Just look at the life in the eyes, the full wet cast of her lips, the almost truculent tilt of her chin and those limbs …" He rammed his hands into his pockets hard. "I wonder if he'll sell it."

She caught Denver by the sleeve and stopped him. "Mr. Chance wants to buy the painting."

Denver blushed. "I … I haven't thought about it …"

"Well," snapped Elton impatiently, "think about it now."

"Well, you know there's the exhibition … I'll have to show it …"

"*What!* Do you mean to stand there and tell me that you intend to exhibit that shameless thing? I'll have the law on you." Mr. Drake was quivering with fury.

"How dare you suggest such a thing," put in Mrs. Drake her livid face ugly and seamed. "It is not enough that you unveil it here in public before … these … these … creatures. Now you speak of exhibiting it …"

"Madam, I do not know who you are," came a clarion voice, "but pray do not be an ass. The creator of this painting has no right, either moral or esthetic, to keep it hidden. It would be a crime against humanity, even as would the destruction of the Mona Lisa."

"Oh, golly, it's the Professor," breathed Favra. "Isn't he magnificent?" He was indeed, arrayed in faultless evening dress, his white mustache clipped to micrometric exactitude, a beribboned pair of pince nez spectacles on his nose. He instantly commanded the attention of the crowd.

Aaron, who had sponsored the idea of making a critic of the Professor, said, "Whoever you are, sir, allow me to take your hand. I agree heartily. No man should create something like this and hide it." He glared at the Drakes. "I understand you are her parents. In spite of that, allow me to compliment your profound and aggressive stupidity."

"Who are you, sir?" Mr. Drake asked the Professor, recovering from the twin attacks and ready for more.

The old man peered through his pince nez as though examining a hairy worm.

"What good would the information do you?" he snorted. "However, I may say I am a patron and a critic of the arts. I am Melton H. Bainbridge, a name which is not entirely unknown in this city."

Favra realized with something like prescience that the closely guarded name of the Professor was now public knowledge, and it was apparent that the name had made the desired impression. Mrs. Drake changed countenance with such rapidity that onlookers felt it must have hurt. Melton Bainbridge passed on through to get a closer look, pausing only long enough to allow Favra to make the conventional introduction, nodded briefly once and approached the picture where he stood a long time gazing at it. From time to time he would let go an exclamation loud enough to be heard by those who pressed closer and closer. Finally he spun around and said to Denver, "Sir, you are the artist?"

Denver, to whom the arrival of Bainbridge was as much a surprise as it was to anyone, nodded.

"Then I stand prepared to buy this painting. What are you asking?"

"Well…" He seemed unable to get the procession of events straight in his mind. "As I told Mr. Chance, I will have to exhibit it and…"

The other waved a casual hand. "Of course, of course. No one in their right mind," he cast a withering glance at the Drakes, "would deny you that. Nevertheless, after you have exhibited it I should like to be the first to make an offer. I stand ready as authorized by my organization to offer you ten thousand dollars for it."

Elton Chance, his face red with anger, stepped forward. "I'll double that."

Aaron who was having trouble with his respiration due to his efforts to abort a scream of mirth and joy stepped into the breach. "Let us not turn what was a party into a commercial bartering bee. I suggest that Mr. Dawson exhibit the painting when and wherever he chooses and then bids will be in order. Right now suppose we return to our merrymaking."

Favra squeezed the Professor's hand and whispered. "You were absolutely earth-shaking. You can go whenever you choose." He drew her aside. "Nonsense. I haven't been this well-dressed or so lionized in thirty years. I'm going to stay and have fun."

"That's fine but suppose you touch only lightly on painting. You've done your part."

His smile was forgiving and joyous. "On the contrary I shall circulate and make encompassing statements about painting, all very much to the point."

"But do you think that safe?"

"I shall confide in you another secret. I have paintings in several important collections and one is in the Royal Palace in Stockholm. My stag hunt was so realistic that good old King Gus fell in love with it and bought it. He was a great hunter you know."

Favra felt that she had taken about all the shocks she could endure so she sat down and watched the little man mingle with the guests. Mr. and Mrs. Drake, firmly put in their places, sat down and remained quiet. Leslie even struck up a conversation with Lucy St. Dennis after finding that Lucy cultivated flowers, as it was a hobby of his.

Borden, sitting a little behind Favra said, "Let's get the hell out of here."

"Oh, no, not yet. The night's young."

Under the cover of the shadow which partially covered them he performed certain magic that made her face pink. "Oh ... all right. You talked me into it. Let's go."

They walked slowly down Royal Street with its musty antique shops, pet shops and bars, holding hands like young lovers.

He sighed audibly. "Do you think this life will bore you, darling?"

"Never," she breathed. "There is a security about marriage that lovers never know. I loved you as a lover, Borden. As my husband I worship you."

"You've associated with Aaron too long. You always beat me with words."

There were a number of people in Favra's apartment but she was not among those present. Aaron Festival walked up and down on the white carpet, his hands behind his back. Seated were Denver Dawson, Melton and Antoinette Bainbridge who now would not be recognized because with her shapeless clothes had gone the crone. She was a well-fleshed, well-preserved woman of fifty, her face jolly, and now that her teeth were replaced, plump and happy. Her clothes were restrained but smart, well-fitting. T'ling hovered in the background serving drinks to everyone who wanted them, looking toward the door now and again, afraid her mistress would come back before they were ready for her. Aaron paused and placed his hand on Esta's shoulder.

"I have asked you all to come here tonight for the purpose of making a collective bow in the dust at the feet of the most wonderful woman I have ever known. I apologize to the rest of my friends when I say that. I feel they will understand what I mean." Esta's hand closed over his in assurance.

"All of us here, in one manner or several, owe Favra McMullin Chance more than we can ever repay. She came here admittedly to live her own life in the way she saw fit. Doubtless to her relatives it seemed the pinnacle of selfishness. I need ask no one here for a refutation of that. I doubt that any of us have ever known anyone who was further from it, unless one wishes to say that she *desired* to do what she did. That is true, but by the same token there is no such thing as true unselfishness. To me she has been a good friend, she was directly instrumental in bringing Esta and me together. To Mr. and Mrs. Bainbridge she has been unfailingly kind, watchful over their well being, and always concerned when all was not well with them. To Denver

Dawson she has meant even more. She handed him a slice of life when it didn't seem important that he live. Furthermore, and at the same time, she handed him one of creation's truly beautiful women, by whose nimble wits Denver was elevated to the plane that had been intended for him all along." Denver's hand sought his wife's and both their eyes were moist.

"Since Arden was hothoused previous to her pilgrimage into the lusty if sometimes smelly air of life, she could probably measure the extent of Favra's generosity with greater accuracy than the rest of us."

"I can measure it, Aaron," she said simply, "but I cannot describe it."

"You have just done so, much better than I have in all my words. Simplicity is a virtue that seldom changes. You brought the picture, Denver?"

Denver fumbled with a huge package, and with nervous fingers managed to unwrap it.

Aaron smiled as the picture came from its coverings. "I shall at this moment arrogate some of the credit for this job. I stole the photograph from which it was copied and supplied some questionable assistance in its birth."

Denver held up the big painting, indrawn breaths and silence were applause enough. It was a bust painting of Favra looking over her left shoulder. He had caught the pearly translucence of her skin, the tawny gold of her hair and the passionate curve of her lips. Her face carried an expression of gentle tolerant wisdom, a look that seemed to bless all it surveyed.

"Taking further liberties, I put a nail in the wall at the street end of the living room. I had to do so because this frame is so much heavier than the Delaire that a heavier support was needed. Melton, if you will be so kind as to remove the Delaire, I shall hang Mrs. Chance in the place of honor." The Professor hastened to take the picture down and Aaron standing on a foot stool provided by T'ling, hung the magnificent portrait in its place.

Outside on the fire escape from which the drama in the living room could be both heard and seen, Favra clung to Borden, tears wetting a large round spot on his blue shirt.

"Besides making a shambles of my shirt," he said with infinite gentleness, "you're playing hob with your makeup. We can go in now."

She nodded and the pain in her throat made her breath uneven and fluttery. "Yes…let's go in. I love every one of them…and they love me…I'm glad I know."

"It's always nice to know," he said stroking her hair. They turned and walked down the steel steps toward the street entrance of the apartment.

THE END

Printed in Great Britain
by Amazon

46633665R00109